High-Water Mark

High-Water Mark

Nicole Dixon

The Porcupine's Quill

Library and Archives Canada Cataloguing in Publication

Dixon, Nicole, 1974–
    High-water mark/Nicole Dixon.

Short stories.
ISBN 978-0-88984-356-1

    I. Title.

PS8607.196H44 2012   C813'.6   C2012-904623-X

1   2   3   ·   14   13   12

Published by The Porcupine's Quill, 68 Main Street, PO Box 160,
Erin, Ontario NOB 1TO. http://porcupinesquill.ca

Edited for the press by Chandra Wohleber.

Represented in Canada by the Literary Press Group.
Trade orders are available from University of Toronto Press.

We acknowledge the support of the Ontario Arts Council and the
Canada Council for the Arts for our publishing program. The financial
support of the Government of Canada through the Canada Book Fund is
also gratefully acknowledged.

Canada
Ontario
Ontario Media Development
Corporation

Canada Council   Conseil des Arts
for the Arts   du Canada

ONTARIO ARTS COUNCIL
CONSEIL DES ARTS DE L'ONTARIO

———

For Darryl Whetter,
who invited me to his blue house
and built me a room of my own.

Contents

High-Water Mark

My sister thinks I gave my mom cancer. Lauren's become an expert on death since her baby died.

I heard *hemorrhoid* when my mom said *thyroid*. I was almost laughing except Lauren started crying, so I realized it wasn't hemorrhoids, even though she cries at everything now. I decided I wasn't gonna sit on that couch with my sister and watch my mom's eyebrows and eyelashes spill out of her face. My mom saw me looking at Lauren and then at her and back at Lauren, and she said, 'You have something to say, Ainslee?'

'I'm going to Robbie's.' And I went to my room, grabbed some shit and left.

I have a summer job in the gift shop up at the Cape. The Cape's a big cliff way up high and way out in the water and way far away from town. I had to buy a truck — a blue-and-white Ford — to get myself up there and back, but mostly Robbie drives it since he's twenty-five and has a licence and I can't get my beginner's yet. Robbie *had* a licence, I should say.

The gift shop looks like a lighthouse and it's the first thing the tourists see when they park their big, shiny American SUVs and all their kids pile out like clowns and squeeze into the shop. They ask if this is the lighthouse they've driven all this way to see and I say, no, the real one's down that hill and they unfold the folded T-shirts with their ice cream fingers and shuffle the postcards and stink up the bathroom and grumble about the drive up the road, like it's personally *my* responsibility to pave it, even though it's the first time they've *really* used their SUVs. And then they complain about having to walk down the hill and ask, can they drive? and ask, could I take their picture? and ask, how much are the T-shirts? and ask, do I see many whales? and ask, what do I do around here for fun?

Tourism's a verbal assembly line.

No, you can't drive, you should walk, Fatso, and I'll tell you the price of T-shirts if you're actually gonna buy one. And for fun? I smoke and drive fast and drink beer and get stoned and fuck Robbie.

'I hike the beach and watch for whales and pick wildflowers.'

'Wish I lived your life.' They sigh.

Sometimes when Robbie remembers to pick me up, we do hike down to the beach — and drink beer he's brought and watch the riptide rip at the rocks. The waves crash higher than our heads and we're soon soaked and freezing but screaming and smashing our bottles into the wind. The rocks are flat and curved like worn stairs, and once Robbie pulled me into a kinda cave and lifted me up onto a ledge. I wrapped my legs around him as he yanked down my jeans and we never noticed the tide coming in until we were done and Robbie's feet were soaked. We had to slip and slide back up the rocks. We sat for a bit while the tide swallowed our little love nest. My dad drowned in those rips, and that's how quick it must have happened — a blink of breath, then lobster bait.

At night, driving off the Cape, there's this one curve where you can see the lights of the village and, just right there, Refugee Cove looks like a glittery city, all lit up for a party. Then down we go to the main road, to Robbie's, pulling into his driveway. That moment is when his house most looks like a trailer, which is exactly what it is.

Lauren calls me Robbie's little woman but living with him feels like one long sleepover. Pyjama drama, pillow fighting.

Lauren's over, trying to be my mom 'cause Mom won't be my mom and Lauren wants so bad to be a mom.

'Why don't you come home?'

'I am home.'

'You're getting stupider. Sunbathing naked on that boat? With all those guys?'

'Robbie was there. It wasn't all day, and I was just topless. *They* were topless. Some of those guys have bigger tits than me.'

'This is what's making her sick.'

I look where Lauren's looking, at my feet on the coffee table, beside my math textbook, some rolling papers, pot crumbs. Robbie's smells like the last slurps of week-old beer in the bottom of a bottle, and there's plenty of that around.

'Robbie got me to quit smoking.'

'Smoking's better for you than Robbie.'

'I'm not making her sick.'

'You're not helping.'

'You get cancer, you get cancer. What I'm doing has nothing to do with it.'

'I think you're wrong. If you're happy, and a good person, good stuff happens. You surround yourself with crap, crap happens. Her being happy could get her better.'

'Is that what you believe? That being happy and good will get you a new life? Then how come Dad's dead? I don't mean people who are good have bad things happen. I mean, people who are good maybe aren't so good.'

The world doesn't need any more people, so it picks at them like scabs and off they go. Yeah, Refugee Cove could stand a few more kids so the school doesn't shut down. I could barely tell Lauren was pregnant at her graduation — she just looked fat under her gown. If they need kids, outside Refugee Cove, there's plenty. Spend some time with me at the gift shop. The way parents yell at or ignore their kids? Makes them seem like black-flies.

No one knew Lauren's kid's heart was fucked until the baby was born. I was an aunt for six days. I liked being Aunt Ainslee; I had plans to make those the kid's first words.

After her kid died, Lauren packed all the baby stuff into a box and left it at the end of her driveway. I poked around at all the toys and bottles and books and clothes while I was waiting for the bus, which appeared just when I found the teeny, yellow toque she wore in the hospital, so I grabbed it and shoved it in my jacket pocket and hopped on the bus. All morning I kept thinking about all that little, little stuff that'd had such big, big plans, so I skipped school at lunch but by the time I got home the box was gone.

When I moved into Robbie's I took that toque with me. Sometimes when Robbie's sleeping I put it on my left hand like a mitten. It barely covers my palm, not even halfway.

The one time I held my niece, her head rested right there in my palm. Lauren still hadn't given her a name, and never did, but when the baby opened her eyes, it was like she was asking for one.

Robbie smoked me up before work today. I can't tell if time's moving faster or slower or if the T-shirts are cold or wet.

Vince is my boss and he's sixty-seven but looks younger than most dads and lives in the woods, where he grows blueberries and weed. What's a bigger deal than his growing weed — since tons of people I know grow weed — is that he moved here from Alberta, when most people from here talk about moving *to* Alberta.

My sister had this job till she got pregnant. I think Vince likes us working here 'cause he fucked my mom years ago. I'm not so sure on that but Lauren used to roll her eyes and make gagging sounds whenever he came around. Lauren remembers Dad more than I do, so it's more of a deal for her.

Vince comes to drop off peanuts and coffee filters and asks, 'Sell anything today, Ainslee?' I can't stop staring at his dirty fingernails. Is he cooking lunch with those?

'I woulda sold a T-shirt if we had greys in extra-large.'

'Two years ago, large was fine. Now it's extra.'

'Busy at the restaurant?'

'Almost outta chowder. Cloudy days aren't BLT days.'

Talk so small you can't see it.

An old guy stumbles in, knee socks and sandals, Tilley hat, Peggy's Cove sweatshirt, large. Especially 'cause Vince is here, I put on my big Cape smile that says *Welcome, Tourist. Yes, we have T-shirts in your size.*

'Can I help you?'

'Oh, ooh. Ha. Where are your restrooms?'

I point to the door beside him.

Good thing Vince raises his voice.

'The bike tour guys are coming later. Can you stay an extra hour to help them bring down their luggage? Cyclone Tours. They've been here before.'

'Cyclops Tours.'

'Hey, Ainslee — no more work weed.'

* * *

Sometimes I get the nervous butterflies, like one day at low tide when Robbie took me out in the truck and we spun doughnuts around in the harbour, red, rotten mud spraying in through the window and all over our faces. It made me laugh like crazy but I got butterflies too. Not just in my stomach — on the tops of my hands and all around my thighs and in the middle of my throat. It's how my mom must feel. Her thyroid's this nervous butterfly in her throat. She wants to swallow it down but it's fucked up her swallowing so it's gotta become a part of her breathing until it gets too big and she can't even breathe anymore.

Tourists are like that — cancer cells. They don't belong and they fuck up the places they visit.

I never want to be a tourist, never want to just watch the riptides; I want to learn how to swim with them.

The Cyclops catches up with me. Cyclone Tours are regular three-season customers so we've shot the shit before. I think he's plucked his monobrow.

'Looking forward to September?' he asks.

'First it's tourists, then hurricanes.'

Robbie has my truck and he's late, so Cyclops and I are footing brick-heavy luggage down to the guest house instead of four-wheel driving. These cyclists freaking *biked* here, they've got the muscles, but it's the gift-shop girl who's bricklaying.

'I always meant to ask what happened to the girl who worked here last summer.'

'She's my sister and she had a baby.'

Cyclops hits a loose rock and nearly drops the luggage.

'She had a baby?'

'Yeah, but it died.'

Then he does fall, him and the luggage down flat. Nothing cracks open, no blood. My hands are too full to help him but I pause and watch. He's backstroking through the dust, then he twists around like a beetle and he's got the luggage and he's suddenly ahead of me.

'She still in town?' he yells. He's marching his cyclist calves.

'Where else would she go?'

We reach the end of the path. It opens like the jaw of a beast, all waves and sky and rowdy wind. Over the valley, black clouds are choking the sun.

'I'm stunned.' Cyclops eyes the edge.

Vince calls people like Cyclops 'repeats'. The year-five honeymooners. The groupies. We like them, not only 'cause they bring us gifts, offerings for the view, but because they know you can't keep this landscape in a frame. They come back for the high, the shock. Each trip, they need to touch the fire to remember it's hot.

But there are the others, the ones who'll see those storm clouds and blame us for the rain and the roads it'll soon turn to gullies. So I'm glad when I see Robbie driving down in my truck, though too fast for the rutted road, aiming straight for us.

'How come you're pissed and won't let me drive?'

'Why were you talking to Bike Boy?'

'I meant drunk pissed. Lauren and I call him Cyclops.'

The rain is crazy loud on the roof of the truck so it sounds like we're fighting before we are.

'Lauren fucked the monster,' he says.

We're driving under water.

'Fuck off, no way.'

'He was hitchhiking to the Cape sometime last October not too far from your mom's, so I give him a ride. Says, "You know Lauren McPhee?" "Yeah, she's my buddy's girlfriend. Going to meet him now at his camp. Why?" I ask. All he says is he didn't know she had a boyfriend. Says nothing the rest of the way. I drop him off at the gift shop and he says it again. Then he gets out, says, "Sorry." Holds his hands up like "don't shoot", closes the door. Don't see him again till now.'

'Last October ...' — I stop to think — 'was around when we found out about Mom.' My thighs are fluttering. 'But so what? It wasn't me, it wasn't you, it's between Lauren and Mike.'

'And their kid if it *was* Mike's.'

'She's dead and you're driving too fast.'

'Slut could run in the family.'

'Fuck off, Robbie. Robbie!'

The truck's sliding instead of driving. It's the last hill before Refugee Cove except I can't see Refugee Cove, just the edge of the Cape, then nothing, nothing's out my window, the front tire's going over except there's a tree, and we stop. I am a quivering insect.

'Ainslee?'

Gravity's outside my door. I crawl over Robbie, straddle him. He leans to my neck, lips puckering to kiss or puke, but I lean farther and open his door, jump out, start walking home. Not the trailer. Home home.

Lauren's there, instead of Mom.

'She went in a helicopter.'

I am made of rain. I go to my room to change.

Lauren and I pass the trailer on our way to Halifax the next morning. My truck's in the yard, front end like a punched nose.

By Truro I almost ask Lauren about Cyclops. Then I don't. My niece is dead and soon Mom will be too.

'When it happens,' Lauren's saying, her voice post-storm calm, 'her ashes —'

'Off the Cape. Her and Dad …' Little Sister's crying.

'Will you do it with me?'

Oncoming traffic is steady. Camper vans are stuffed with deflated beach balls, lawn chairs, coolers, families. Licence plates of every colour. It's late August.

From my back pocket I get the yellow toque, pull it over my fingers and hold it up for Lauren to see. Her eyes widen. She takes one hand off the steering wheel and grabs my fingers, bringing them and the toque to her nose, her cheek, her neck, her stomach. Doesn't let go.

Sick Days

The grade-five students are making Mona Berlo ill. January, and she's used up almost one-third (33 percent) of her sick days — home with the flu, a reaction to the flu shot, three colds and a sinus infection. Headaches, dizziness, cramps. Twenty new pounds have bloated her hips and thighs, causing her to bury her size six September dress pants far inside her closet and, when Carl is visiting from university, undress for bed in the dark. The kids are breaking her down. The air in the classroom buzzes with hormones.

'I hate you,' spits Destiny Albert.

Mona is checking the division homework. Incomplete, incorrect, crumpled, stained, reeking of cigarette smoke. No matter how many times they review the work, the same six students understand, bored, as the others fall behind. Destiny, as usual, didn't even take hers home.

'Destiny, that's inappropriate. You know you'll have to stay after school.'

'But I can't!'

Mona doesn't want to stay after school either. The final bell is a release from the gate; when the students scream down the stairwell and tumble on top of one another at three, instead of yelling at them to stay in a line and be quiet, she wants to race past, thrust them aside and launch out the door, into the yard, across the street, dodge traffic and flee, brown curls streaming behind, her students choking and scrambling. She shifts her feet, a curl falling behind her ear. Tucking her clipboard under her arm, Mona twirls a piece of her hair around a finger and squeezes it back into its schoolmarm bobby pin. Her snug white T-shirt rises slightly above her skirt, exposing a small, acute angle of belly. She pulls the T-shirt down and out of her damp armpits. Meets Destiny's slit-green eyes, which glower through her long, blond bangs. The other students murmur and begin to squirm, Friday crazies simmering. Mona turns her big brown eyes wide to Destiny.

'Well, you should have done your homework.'

'I *hate* you!'

Mona's nostrils flare. She taps her black Mary Jane toe on the floor. 'Go stand in the hall.' Destiny is a seated wall, crossed arms tightening, chin lowering into her chest. Mona breathes deeply and tries to relax her shoulders. 'Now.' Destiny scrapes her chair and goes, stomping and huffing. Mona notices as she passes that they are almost the same height — Destiny is a full foot taller than in September. Tony Wang giggles as she reaches the door.

'Shut up! *Shut up!*' Destiny lunges at Tony, grabs his chair and pulls it out from under him. His little body plunges to the floor.

'Destiny!'

She turns to Mona, green eyes wild in her red face, hair thrashing, and flings the chair at her. It misses by half a metre and smashes against the front blackboard, the blue plastic seat detaching from its metal legs in a clamour of bumps and clangs, before settling onto the floor. Mona drops her clipboard, adding to the clatter. She spreads open her fingers, turns her face from the pieces of chair to Tony, his eyes welling, to the other grade fives, most emotionless, some close to laughter, to Destiny, still by the door, body heaving.

'Office. Go to the office.' Mona reaches for the black class phone and begins to dial the number. She turns back to Destiny, the receiver suspended near Mona's ear. 'Now!' Destiny swings the door, creaky on its hinges, then slams it behind her.

This is Mona's first year teaching, her first adulthood months of being on salary, pre-dawn bus commutes, skipped breakfasts and limping (hi honey!) home at the end of the day, brain and body exhausted. Except Mona's adult world is populated by children.

'Hello Miss Berlo.'

'Ms.'

'Right. *Miz.*' Russell Bigney introduced himself during the stuffy, dusty, newly waxed, literal warm-up of dragging and arranging desks, sorting ripped books and sweeping up mouse turds, the last week of searing city August. He teaches grade six across the hall and began at the school around the time his students were born. Russell already looks well into his forties — chalky and stretched, a gin-blossoming nose — though he must be younger. Yet Mona could tell then and sometimes thinks now, he'd once been cute. His oval grey eyes are still reflective and kind, his personality magnetic and eager, when he isn't drained from teaching, which he is, usually, or isn't drinking, which he (and the other teachers) do often.

'I have your class list.' The two teachers squeezed on top of Mona's desk and leaned in to scan the photocopy in Russell's hand; his T-shirt was dimpled with moisture and stained yellow around the neck. He shook his head as he read, his oversized, blue-rimmed glasses sliding down his nose. 'You have a tough group.'

'Debbie told me.'

Russell looked at her. His glasses were smudged. 'Did she tell you the last two teachers who had this class quit? No, principals look out for themselves and their careers. They tell you what's convenient. They got into teaching not to teach but to be the top bully, the enforcer of rules. Ooh.' He whistled, pointing to a name on Mona's roster. 'Do *not* get into a power struggle with Destiny Albert.'

Often with love and relationships, Mona didn't choose, they just happened. But Mona chose Carl. Last year, they lived together in the same student townhouse during her bachelor of ed. and his second year of sociology. Mona watched her roommate try to study on the couch, weighted by the big words in his thick textbook, staring at the space between the living room and the kitchen.

'What are you thinking?' she asked as she stirred her fourth pot of spaghetti that week.

'I can't believe I paid ninety bucks for this book.'

'You gotta wonder how much beer ninety bucks would buy.'

'I don't drink.' Carl turned back to his textbook.

Since Mona had never known anyone who didn't drink — especially at university and especially among her fellow future teachers, who were treating their bachelor of ed. as one last, yearlong party before they had to settle into the lonely alcoholism of adulthood — she realized Carl was more serious and therefore more mature. Tired of dating boys, Mona thought Carl could be the man she needed to accompany her into her new adult life.

On a Friday night, other roommates gone, Mona proposed chicken parmesan and Carl accepted. The townhouse filled with the smell of bubbling cheese and tomato sauce; at the table, Mona's gaze lingered whenever Carl looked at her above the vanilla-scented candle.

'You don't mind if I have some wine?' Mona asked.

Carl shrugged.

'They're your brain cells.'

Later, as Carl did the dishes, Mona hooked her hands quickly on, then off his waist, and he turned, and they kissed, tongues still hungry after dinner. They started to make their way through the townhouse but while Mona was willing to pause on the couch or desk, Carl led a straight line to his bedroom. They were naked fast, he was inside her faster, yet once there he was slow and patient, steady, steady, steady, asking *Like this?* whispering *You feel so good* until she came, and since Mona had never come her first time with anyone else, she took this as a sign. Mona shelved her chin between his shoulder and neck and Carl drew her closer.

Now Mona and Carl see each other most weekends while he finishes his last year of school. They talk nightly on the phone about her current job and his plans of being a cop, but mostly they have nothing to say, the silent dimes-per-minute adding up. In Mona's apartment, they spend a lot of time gaining weight on her couch.

I chose this, Mona has to remind herself. *Isn't this the grown-up life I wanted?*

'I always thought I'd have a large family. You know, maybe three kids. At least two anyway.' Carl rubs Mona's soles as they curl up in front of a rerun of *Friends.* Rachel, pregnant with Ross's baby, feels that at thirty, this is her last chance for children.

'Lucky *you* don't have to squeeze them out.' Mona clenches the tops of her thighs.

'They have drugs you can take —'

'That they inject into your spine and that make your baby stupid.'

'You said you wanted kids?' Carl's eyes shimmer TV blue.

'I've already got thirty-one.'

Like a lot of little girls, Mona had an array of dolls. Yet while many girls played mom or bride, Mona lined up her dolls on the floor and played teacher, wearing out her green chalkboard to an unusable smoothness. After that, Mona turned the board over to the magnetic side and slid her colourful alphabet into hundreds of words.

The kids in the daycare where she worked during high school

thought she knew magic. When Mona transformed red and yellow into orange, every little body crushed into her thighs, paintbrushes sprouts in the air. At storytime, no bums squirmed; no one had to pee. Tears were tickled to laughter and, when she spoke, Mona heard her English echoed in place of their Cantonese, Vietnamese, Portuguese. Her chest growled like a stomach; it wasn't pride but hunger. When they learned she was also filled. All want vanished.

Her B.Ed. was going to be the first bite of a long, satisfying meal. At orientation she met the forty classmates she would accompany to all of her classes, not just pedagogy (which these same classmates pronounced *ped-a-go-geye*) but science, art, even phys. ed.

'Look around,' said Dr Hildenbrand, the music professor. 'You are embarking on your careers and about to meet your lifelong chums. You'll be standing up at one another's weddings!'

'Assuming we get married,' Mona muttered to the scrubbed, bobbed, dyed blonde beside her, before she noticed the platinum marquis setting on her finger.

'Now get up and mingle. Complete the people scavenger hunt! Make sure you introduce yourselves as teachers!' Dr Hildenbrand was like many music teachers: too marching band. Mona looked at her sheet. *Find someone who is over forty! Find someone who's been to Australia! Find the person with the most kids!*

'Have you been to Australia?' Mona asked the blonde.

'No, but, uh, let's see. I know the primary colours. Red, green and blue.'

'They're red, blue and *yellow*,' Mona corrected.

'I know we're expected to teach art,' the blonde said quietly, 'but as if I'm going to. Like it's important.'

'Art helps us think critically. Even helps us do better at math.'

The blonde turned away, then circled something on her sheet.

'Wait. What's your name? Miss —?'

'Ms Berlo.'

Mona, plunked into the middle of her grade-five classroom, used the scavenger hunt like a life preserver on her very first day: *Find someone who's read every Harry Potter book more than once. Find the person with the most brothers and sisters. Find someone who's had chicken pox.*

'Miss?'

'It's Ms Berlo, uh' — Mona looked over her roster — 'Dakota.'

'I'm Destiny.'

'Oh. Of course. I'm sorry. You have a question?' Mona's mouth watered.

'This is gay. Do we have to do it?'

Mona felt emptied, queasy. 'It's fun,' she said weakly. 'You'll get to know one another.'

'But we already know one another,' Destiny said.

'Well I don't. And don't use *gay* like that.'

'*Ogay.*'

By morning recess, most of the teachers have heard of Destiny's thrown-chair tantrum. Some believe it a weakness in teaching. Not moods. Not bad parenting.

'When I had Destiny two years ago,' says Wilt, slurping his stale recess coffee, then resting it on his globe stomach, 'I *never* had problems.'

In the classroom, no, Mona thinks. *But in the bedroom? In the bathroom? With that gut? Problems.*

At lunch hour, the staff room is empty. Mona tries to decompress over a pepperoni slice from the store while staring out the window at the kids' lunch-trudged snow paths. Because of the morning incident, no one has invited her to lunch but does she really want to watch Wilt stuff his overblown gut with a bacon double cheeseburger and fries? Russell interrupts Mona's view.

'Something tells me you'll need a drink tonight.'

'Something, or some*one*?' Mona unwraps her chocolate bar, sucking it slowly from solid to liquid. Russell shrugs, gulping his stewy, reheated leftovers.

'A few of us are going to the Jack and Stone. You should come.' He blinks at Mona's squirming mouth.

'I don't know. Carl'll be in town tonight.'

'When?'

'Later.'

'Tell him to meet us.'

'Okay, okay.' Mona crumples her wrapper, getting up from the sticky table. She has an ancient-Egypt lesson to plan. 'We'll see.' She steps away, then turns. 'Hey, Russ?'

His eyes, she notices, jerk from her ass to her face. 'Yeah?'

'Is your classroom open? Mind if I look through your social studies books?'

Russell fishes through the nylon pockets of his tracksuit. 'Here,' he says, and tosses her his warm keys.

Fridays during the fall, Mona climbed the stairs to her apartment lusting for Carl. As she jangled her keys, Carl would open the door, encase her within his long, hairy arms, then pull her into the apartment. She would barely have dropped her bags before he began kissing her neck, gripped her hair, unbuttoned her shirt and ran his tongue around her chest, back and forth, leaving a bridge of spit between both nipples. She worked at his belt and fly as he led her to the bedroom and onto the bed, where they frantically stripped, sucked, then fucked away a week's worth of work and school tension. Skin yielding, belly slippery from sweat, Mona breathed Carl's scent deeply, smelled the garlic on his fingers from the supper baking in the oven. All weekend they would act out the fantasies they had held in their heads while apart.

As the nights got longer and the light faded, as work and school got busier, as both Mona and Carl started to pack on the pounds, their lust for each other diminished. Last Friday, Mona found Carl not at the door but on the couch, staring, flip, flip, flipping the channels of her TV. Tapping the end of a Pringles can into his mouth, raised for crumbs.

'Carl.' Mona dropped her bags and slumped against the door.

'Yeah?' Carl glanced over his shoulder. 'Hey, good to see you. Sorry I ate all the chips.'

'Did you start supper?'

'In a minute. Or do you want to?'

Mona placed on the empty kitchen table her just-bought bottle of wine, then joined Carl on the couch.

'Do you want to go out tonight?' Mona asked after a peck on Carl's cheek.

'Nah. Let's stay in and rent an action movie. With lots of shooting.'

'Action.' Mona sighed.

TGI Friday once again. By the end of the thrown-chair day Mona is ready to do some drinking with the teachers. She has no desire to go home, no desire to find Carl on the couch again. Forget sex. Get drunk.

Russell and three other teachers are at the Jack with a nearly empty pitcher and a new, full one already on the table. The winter afternoon darkens quickly and the pint glasses are never more than half empty. Mona loses count of pitchers consumed. The other teachers leave one by one and by seven or eight (Mona looks at her watch but keeps forgetting the time) it is just Mona and Russell.

'I sshud Carl. I shhood call Carl.'

'Didn't you already?'

'Didn't I already what?'

Russell leans in, elbows on the splattered table, hot, sour breath close. Even his glasses seem speckled with dried beer. Mona smiles sloppily, swaying.

'I hate teaching,' she whispers, leaning in.

'You had a tough day.'

'A tough year. I won't last three years. I hate them.'

'Who?'

'The kids. Those little shithead assholes. They're barely ten. Why are they assholes already?'

'You doan hate them.'

'I doan wanna teach,' Mona whines.

'You love teaching.' Russell pauses to drain his pint and pour a new one. 'Say, you gonna marry Carl? Is it serious?'

'Oh, evereeone alls asks. Why'd you hafsta ask?'

Russell looks towards the door, then straightens.

''Cause he's coming in the bar right now.'

'Oh jeezus, how'd he known I's here?' Mona ducks her head.

'Didn't you call him?' Russell asks.

'Did I?'

Carl stands at their table for a minute, as though he doesn't want to sit down, before slowly dragging out a chair.

'Hey Carl.' Mona waves. 'When you gonna make an honest teacher outta me?' She snickers.

'How much have you had to drink?' Carl asks.

'Two plus five, carry the one … We'll know when the bill comes.'

'How's school, Carl?' Russell asks.

'Fine. Midterms soon. Mona, we should go.'

'But you're just here.' Mona pouts.

'Stay,' Russell adds. 'We could order wings. Let's get a glass. You sshud get in on this pitcher.'

'I —' Carl starts.

'Oh, Carl doznut drink.' Mona shakes her head.

'Why not?'

Carl looks at Russell.

'My dad was an alcoholic.'

'Ah, right. Where you goin', Moan?'

'Pee. I've gotta pee. N'more.' As she stands, beer sloshes from her glass onto the table, then trickles onto Carl's lap.

'Ohm ssoorry!' She points at Russell, scowling, then pulls at the bottom of her T-shirt. 'N'more, sserioussly. Look at what I didta Carl. Poor Carl.'

'Okay.' Russell grins and Carl frowns.

On the toilet, a hazy blur of naked bodies flutters into Mona's mind. As the images solidify, she realizes it's Russell she's thinking about and she blushes from guilt and excitement. Does she want that? She's never thought about cheating on Carl but suddenly knows that if they're going to be together for a while, she absolutely will. Is that wrong or natural? And is that future Russell? He isn't that cute but he isn't bad, and he is older, maybe he'd know a few more things. There are days, though, at school, when he definitely smells like liquor-store cologne. But in the dark, does it matter whose hands? Whose tongue? Whose skin? She wipes, then forgets to wash her hands. When she opens the bathroom door with her butt, Carl is waiting on the other side.

'Juss like you used to,' she mumbles.

'I was washing my pants. Let's go.' Carl hooks Mona's arm and leads her like a naughty child to the table.

'You going?' Russell asks.

'Looks like it.' Despite her pink cheeks, Mona feels a chill. She searches for her scarf and begins coiling it around her neck, stretching back to tie the knot behind her head. As Carl leaves to get a cab, Russell studies her, eyes even, following her hands, stopping before they reach down for her coat. His gaze, half-lidded, lowers to her sudden nipples. His hands grip and squeeze his pint glass.

The hasty bar exit, the bumpy cab ride, barely spilling out onto the sidewalk in time to puke in the fresh snow, sliding her body along the railing up to her apartment — are all blurry as Mona drops her keys twice outside the door. She forgets about Carl until he reaches to grab the keys. Mona squeezes past Carl's body and starts padding towards the bathroom, hand to her mouth.

'Oh, I gotta barf!'

'You're beyond drunk,' he says, closing the door firmly.

'So drunk.' Mona collapses in front of the toilet, grateful for once that the seat is up. Carl comes to the door.

'I'm going to bed.'

'So sick,' Mona bleats. 'Water?' But Carl is gone.

After dozing on the bathroom floor, Mona drags a bucket beside the bed, throwing up until her stomach empties. She dreams of Destiny, walking along holding her hand, then letting go and running from her, tripping.

She spends most of her Saturday in bed, getting up to gulp water and orange juice, wait for the Brita to fill, take Advil. Always, Carl is on the couch watching hockey or reruns. Silent. Late afternoon, she sits beside him.

'I had a bad day yesterday,' she starts.

'You always have a bad day.'

'Destiny threw a chair at me.'

'Someday I might get shot at.'

'Someday I might too.'

Carl turns down the volume, though he doesn't need to.

'What the hell were you thinking, getting that drunk with that fucking guy?'

'What are you talking about? We've gone out drinking before. There were other teachers there.'

'Not when I got there. You both looked pretty guilty. This is why I don't drink. People do such stupid things when they drink.'

'There're lots of reasons you don't drink. And if you did, maybe it'd loosen you up.'

'So you go drink with Russ to "loosen up"? Nice.'

'Oh Christ, I'm still too sick to fight. There is no point in fighting about this. Russell is my *co*-worker and a *friend*. Nothing else. I want to hang out with him 'cause he actually knows the hell I'm going through. He's been teaching for over ten years, he's had some of my students. I feel like I can't talk about work with you 'cause you seem so damned bored or you don't understand. Most of the time whatever's on TV is more interesting. I try to complain and you just say "You're complaining too much." Well it sucks sometimes and I've gotta bitch.'

'When you went to the bathroom, Russell nudged me and said, "Hey, Mona's tits look great in that shirt." This is the guy you wanna get drunk with?'

'Are you serious? Did you agree?'

'I just went to get you in the bathroom. Look, if you want to do this as your career, you're going to have to avoid being so negative. You're starting to get all wrinkly.'

'Oh thank you so fucking much.'

'I'm telling you that 'cause you're my girlfriend. I do want to help. Drinking isn't going to help.'

'If I keep teaching I'm sure I'll still drink sometimes.'

'Well, how about if you want to drink, you could think about me — give me a call or something — can you try and I'll try to listen?'

'Right. Okay.'

The practicum schools had limited spaces so Mona found herself doubled into a grade-one classroom with Tori, the engaged blonde.

'I wish I could get the kids to call me Mrs Ducharme now. They can't even pronounce *Miss Kusmierczyk*.'

'Why don't you try Ms K?' Mona suggested.

'I don't know. *Miz* just sounds so ... *lesbian*.'

The first day, Tori brought cupcakes with silver sprinkles. 'Peanut-free!'

Mona brought only her notebook. Despite the encouragement of their supervising teacher, (Mrs) Edwina Pirzada, to sit and observe, Tori continuously wanted to photocopy, wipe noses, accompany Edwina on yard duty. At recess, Mona watched through the window as Tori chased the grade ones around the jungle gym. During lunch, the two student teachers sat together in the staff room.

'I love kids.' Tori beamed. 'My fiancé and I want four. We're gonna start right away so I still have my body. How about you?'

'I don't think I want kids.' Mona bit into her turkey sandwich.

'Really? Sure you do. You have a boyfriend. You're going to be a teacher. Great maternity benefits. You could keep having babies and take years off. Paid.' Tori leaned forward and her voice lowered. 'Listen, Mona. You should really get more involved. You'll need a good evaluation from Edwina to get a job.'

'But it's only the first day. Besides, I don't feel the need to be another woman who's gotta *prove* she's good with kids. I *know* I am. Right now I want to learn.'

Tori shrugged. 'Okay, but it's a tight job market and, so far, who do you think will get the better evaluation?'

Mona avoided Tori after that, and Tori sat with the other female teachers at lunch, copies of Tori — glossy and squeaky and glassy-eyed — who talked about shopping while twisting their engagement rings or rubbing their not-yet-showing pregnant bellies.

'I know!' Tori cried one day. 'It is *so* hard to plan a wedding during teacher's college!'

Carl's hard-on pulsing into her ass wakes Mona sometime after one. He reaches down the front of her pyjamas and rolls her nipple between his thumb and finger.

'Ouch.' Mona squirms away as Carl begins yanking at her pyjama bottoms. 'I'm so tired.'

'You'll wake up.'

'And still kinda dizzy. Is my forehead hot? I think it's hot.'

'You're always off.'

'We're off. Why are we always off? I just don't feel like screwing now. I'm not faking. I haven't been.'

'I hope not. Sick and otherwise.'

Most parents, unwilling to parent, thrust their kids back to school the second they think they're no longer contagious. By mid-autumn, Edwina's grade ones were going through a box of tissues a day. Mona emptied her pockets nightly of moist white-and-green wads, washing her hands raw. Before morning exercises, she noticed Grady struggling with his jacket by the closets at the back of the room.

'I'll help you, Grady.' He had just returned from his chicken pox quarantine and seemed thinner, the reddish-black scabs like marker drawn on his pale skin. Mona squatted to fiddle with his caught zipper.

'I have one down there, Miziss Blurblo.'

'Really.' Mona kept yanking at the nylon in the zipper's teeth. His hand brushed her cheek as he reached into his pants.

'See?'

She looked to her left. In Grady's hand, centimetres from her nose, was his tiny pink penis, tipped with one red chicken pock. Apple-juice smell of pee. Mona scuttled backwards.

'Wow, Grady, I hope it's not itchy.'

'Not anymore.'

She freed his jacket and, standing, almost patted his greasy, brown hair.

'Okay. Put it away and go wash your hands.'

'Carl. Hey, Carl!' He slowly pushes open the bathroom door to find Mona, her pyjama top unbuttoned, standing on the toilet, looking in the vanity mirror. 'Look.' Carl tries to study her stomach, though his eyes keep sliding to her breasts. 'Stomach.' Mona points.

'I'm sorry I said you looked old. You look good.'

'Ugh. I've got chicken pox. It makes sense.'

'You've had them?'

Mona steps down from the toilet. 'No, I never got them. Which is crazy. During my grade-one practicum there was an epidemic and I thought, maybe I'm immune. But I've been sick, right? Lowered immune system.'

'Still, it could be, I don't know, a rash?' Carl says. Mona looks at him.

'Okay, officer. I've had a fever. I've been dizzy and achy. I woke up itchy. Now look.' She points to five small boils on her stomach. 'I'm contagious.'

'I had them as a kid.'

'I can call in sick!'

Mona and Carl take a cab to the hospital, where they are immediately sealed into a private room. When the doctor enters almost two hours later, he reads the chart, then looks at Carl.

'You can wait outside.'

'But I'm her boyfriend.'

The doctor looks at Mona.

'Please wait outside,' he states.

'I'll be right outside,' Carl says.

'Sure.'

'He's had chicken pox?' the doctor asks as the door closes.

'Yeah. So it *is* chicken pox?'

The doctor nods, placing his cold stethoscope on the top of Mona's left breast. She feels the chill in her nipple.

'You'll have to take at least a week off work. You work?'

'I teach grade five.'

'Ah. Do you have any children?'

Mona snorts.

'No. Why?'

'Well, if you want any in the future, you should be aware that chicken pox can cause sterility in adults.' He scribbles a prescription and hands it to her. 'Make sure you take these pills and you should be fine.' She looks at the prescription, the doctor's scratch much like her students' handwriting.

'So, if I miss a couple, I may not be able to have kids?'

'That's a possibility.' The doctor begins to shuffle from the room, and opens the door.

'Maybe I should miss a couple,' Mona mutters as Carl, anxious as an expectant dad, appears at the door.

'Destiny, what's your destiny?' During a late-autumn detention, Destiny was staring, neck arched back, at the spitballs she'd attached to the ceiling.

'I wanna be a model.'

'Well, you'll be tall enough. But you're also a great reader. There's a lot you could do.' Mona was marking at her desk. She looked up at Destiny, who seemed smaller alone in the classroom, the child she was supposed to be.

'I don't wanna be a teacher.'

'You don't have to be, but I wanted to be a teacher.' Mona realized she sounded defensive. 'I like seeing you learn. I know that school, lots of stuff can be tough. Can suck. I want you all to know that learning doesn't have to suck. You can like it, want to learn, know it's fun and keep wanting to do it. Do you ever think about going to college or university?'

'I dunno.' Destiny was tearing apart her pink eraser. 'Do I hafta, to be a model?'

'Destiny, sure, be a model. But how long can you be one? Till you're twenty-five? Twenty-eight? Then what?'

Destiny shrugged, her face twisting like her eraser.

'By then I'll be old anyway.'

'I'm twenty-five,' Mona said.

After her twenty minutes, Destiny bolted from the classroom without putting up her chair. Mona went to her desk and brushed eraser bits to the floor, where she found that night's homework sheet, creased and dirty. She sighed.

A few days later, Mona was filing the December report cards into her students' school records. She began reading through their psychological reports and behaviour plans. In grade two, after Destiny's parents' divorce, she'd jump onto her desk and get on all fours to bark and neigh. Gyrate during 'O Canada'. Spit on her teacher. Her teacher at the time? Weighty Wilt. Mona looked at Destiny's collage of class photos from kindergarten to grade five. Various lengths of hair. The grade-one bowl cut. By grade three, her gummy smile was replaced by dark under-eye circles, the same shadows that had only just begun to darken Mona's eyes.

At home, Mona went through her own class photos. Fat cheeks graduated to pimples. Looking closely at her own grade-five picture, she noticed her brown eyes had hints of green, were almost hidden by her long, dark-blond bangs. Here was Destiny, fifteen years earlier.

The next time Carl mentioned having kids, Mona asked if he ever thought about the terrible twos, temper tantrums, breasts at six, periods by eight?

'Don't you worry about backtalk, birth defects, learning disabilities?'

'Our kids will be different.' He smiled, rubbing Mona's feet.

'How do you know?'

'I just know.'

Carl could think he knew because he wasn't a cop yet. Hadn't yet been in kids' houses, seen their lives, listened, as Mona had, to their parents' pleas for help. *She won't do her homework. He doesn't listen. She does what she wants. I've tried everything.*

'Carl —'

'Hmm?'

'Never mind.' Why burst his bubble? As convinced as Carl was that their kids would be good and happy, Mona thought otherwise. Her school photos, so strangely similar to Destiny's, proved kids weren't different. Or were, in unexpected ways.

When reminding herself that she had chosen Carl, Mona also had to convince herself that she wanted his kids. But was it Carl's kids she didn't want, or anyone's, including her own?

After the hospital, Carl leaves for school and Mona breaks the news to her principal. Then calls Russell.

'I have chicken pox.'

'Scratch and win.'

'A Destiny-free classroom and I'm at home.'

'She hasn't been suspended.'

'Are you serious?'

'Yeah, they don't suspend kids anymore. Swearing, fighting, graffiti, chairs. Parents can't watch them, don't want to. Too much paperwork for the principals. She'll be in the office Monday, back in your class Tuesday. If she went home, she'd watch TV. She's gotta pull a knife.'

'You wondered why I hate this?'

'No. But it's a job. Jobs suck. Would you rather work through the summer? Sit in a windowless cubicle all day, handcuffed to a computer, only get up to pee and talk about TV and shopping at the water cooler?'

'Like the staff room's different. But wait, you mean, there are jobs where I could pee when I want?' Mona laughs.

'Not eat lunch when a bell rings?'

'Grab a needed snack and not have thirty-one pairs of hungry eyes staring at you as you chew?'

'Sit down? Work somewhere that doesn't smell like puke or shit? Work with adults?'

'Adults *are* children. It's too upside down. The kids have adult problems and I've got a childhood disease.'

'You're off work, paid. Destiny-free.'

'Think she'll miss me? Her aim will go down without the practice.'

'We'll all miss you.'

Russell is quiet for a long time. Some of the night at the Jack is coming back to Mona.

'I have pox inside my bathing suit area,' she says into the phone, grinning. Mona thinks she hears something drop.

'I should go. Hope you come back soon.'

On the last day of their practicum, Edwina conferenced separately with

Mona and Tori, Tori before school and Mona after. They said their good-
byes at the end of the day.

'How did it go, Tori?'

'Glowing.'

Mona sat across from Edwina at her desk. Yellow chalk rimmed the
cuffs of Edwina's blue blouse and was embedded in the cracks of her fingers. Mona looked at her own hands, then wiped them on her pants.

'You have a good rapport with the students. They seem to trust you.'

The grade ones had made her a card. On the cover was a drawing of
Mona: square-bodied, a big, red, one-line smile, crayon-brown hair, black-
marker Mary Janes. Glitter on her sweater. Tori, she noted, had no glitter
on her card. And her head looked a lot like a cupcake.

'You need to remember, though, that they are just kids. Your vocabu-
lary is often too adult, too strong. When you talk to the kids, it's not the
same as talking to an adult. You could use a different tone of voice. Softer,
higher, gentler. Like Tori.'

'Ah.'

'Tori will be a great primary teacher. Maybe you'd be better at a higher
grade. Five and up. Or sub for a while. You're too aggressive for this age.'

'But I don't know if they should be babied.'

'They *are* babies.'

'They grab one another's crotches in the schoolyard.'

'Because they see that on TV. Don't be difficult. To be a teacher,
you'll have to learn to join and blend. You could have helped out with one
of our sports teams, sat in on some committees or joined in conversations
more in the staff room. Got your head out of your books. A school works
best as a team.'

'But I sat one-on-one with some of the kids, we read, they said they
really liked that. And I read 'cause I enjoy it but also to model —'

'Once you have your own classroom, you'll never have time for that. It
doesn't look as good and it's not as visible as fundraising or coaching vol-
leyball. Really, what's the use of all that time spent reading to just one
child?'

That night, Mona sobbed into Carl's chest.

'Nothing's going right! I won't get a job!'

'At least we're going right,' Carl said, and Mona kept crying.

* * *

When she returns to work, Mona worries that whatever thin authority she had over her students will have rotted like milk forgotten in a fridge during a vacation. Yet as she rounds the corner to her classroom, she sees her door covered in construction-paper cards.

'Aww, they did miss you,' Russell gushes, coming out of his classroom.

'You or the sub put them up to this.'

'Actually, no.'

'Really?'

'You know, as little as you think you're doing for them, you are the most stable thing in a lot of their lives.'

'Person, place *and* thing.' Mona unlocks her door, drops her bag beside her desk and sits down. On top is a large black construction-paper star with silver gel-pen swirls. Opening the card, she reads: *Your back,* ♥ Destiny. More stars drawn all around. Though Mona had yelled at Destiny for scribbling stars all over her notebooks, Mona had taught the class how to draw those stars.

Friday night, waiting on her couch for Carl, Mona realizes she is no longer afraid to dump him. She began this relationship thinking she needed stability. What does stable mean? Mona had thought support — Carl's chest when she cried, someone to listen. But does stable, does being an adult, also have to mean being boring?

For Carl, stable means a centrally heated home, a rented movie with parents and kids under blankets. Gaining weight, diminished interest in sex — this is part of Carl's stable life, and therefore fine. For Mona, it's not fine. She doesn't want this boring life. She doesn't want to be fat. She wants to lose weight and keep having sex. And she knows she won't if she stays with Carl.

Mona hears the rattle of Carl's keys and gets up from the couch, ready to meet him at the door.

Afternoon yard duty and Mona doesn't mind. The asphalt schoolyard is bleached with mid-winter light; she has given up yelling at kids to put their coats back on. She paces the junior yard, one hand inside a big brass bell. Russell walks towards her.

'Not your yard duty and you're outside?' Mona asks.

His face is concern.

'You and Carl broke up?'

'I knew I wouldn't have to tell you.'

'You okay?'

'Absolutely.'

'So I brought you this for nothing?' Russell holds out half a day-old doughnut, its grease already clear stains on the napkin.

'Oh, no thanks.'

Russell shrugs, and eats. They watch the schoolyard, a blur and yelp of colourful students.

'What are your girls up to?' Russell nods at a giggling cluster.

'I don't know. This last week they started bringing their dolls to school. They probably haven't played with them in a couple of years. They kinda laugh about it, then pass them around, talk in baby voices. Like they're being ironic but clinging suddenly to something. Most of them have gotten their periods.'

'Are the boys teasing them about the dolls?'

'Not really. At first, a bit, but the girls were pretty tough about it, so the boys went back to their soccer.'

'No dolls for Destiny.'

'She's got a book.' Destiny sits on a sun-dried spot of bench, bent into her novel, oblivious to the screaming yard.

'Do you want to go for a drink later?' Russell asks, smiling back towards the school.

'No. I've got tons of marking to do. I'm behind on my plans.'

'Have a glass of wine, though,' Russell calls.

'Oh, I will.'

When the bell rings, Mona clangs her own bell, fierce at the end of her wrist. The students awake from their games and begin to file into squirming lines. Destiny runs to Mona.

'Miss, can I ring the bell?'

'If you ask properly.'

Destiny rolls her green eyes.

'*Ms* Ber*lo*, may I *please* ring the bell?'

'Sure.' Mona, holding the clapper, hands the bell to Destiny, who seizes the wooden handle and, with her whole wild body, grinning dramatically, begins pealing into the corners of the yard a resounding, clear toll that sings as bright and electric as the winter sun.

Saudade

Her name is Jette. Short for Jocasta. Her parents, she says, are Greek and tragic. She tells Ingrid and Sabine that sometimes her band, Martian Barn, doesn't rock enough for her. She says she misses the company of women. When she leaves their table for the bathroom, Sabine turns to Ingrid and licks her lips. Ingrid nods, staring after Jette's vapour trail.

During Martian Barn's second song, their shut-up-and-listen song, Jette gets up from behind her keyboard, grabs the lead guitarist's mike and charges centre stage. She is solid — her body tough in a rip-sleeved T-shirt, her dark brown hair asymmetrically layered, her slightly distorted voice in harmony with the fuzzy, frenzied guitars. Ingrid and Sabine have heard many lead female singers' tiny voices get drowned out by the instruments in their mostly male bands but Jette's voice is an engine.

At their table afterwards, waiting for Jette, Ingrid says, 'We need a change, but is this what we want?'

'How can I say no?' asks Sabine.

Ingrid eyes Sabine suspiciously.

'Don't you mean *we*?'

They met at a party over a year ago. Ingrid found herself, as she often did at most parties, near the stereo or computer, perusing the host's music collection.

'Uh-oh. Another stereo Nazi,' were the first words Sabine said to Ingrid. Ingrid turned around. In front of her was a tiny but scrappy, bobbed and black-haired Sabine in bright green tights and matching blazer. Sabine smiled as she introduced herself. So did Ingrid.

'I'm impressed he's got CDs,' Ingrid said. 'Most parties I find a computer patched into the stereo, songs on totally random, anti-party shuffle.'

'I fucking hate MP3s,' Sabine said.

'Me too. Okay, convenient, yes —'

'Yes.'

'But play a CD, or, better yet, vinyl on a good stereo and it'll blow your mind. You can actually hear every instrument.'

'You have a good stereo?' Sabine finished her beer.

'Well, my dad —'

'Lemme guess. Your dad switched to MP3s and —'

'Now I have a good stereo.'

The women laughed.

'I need another drink.' Sabine looked at Ingrid's empty hands. 'You? Sure you do.'

Ingrid followed Sabine into the kitchen, then back to the living room. There, squeezed but settled onto a couch, the women's conversation ranged from favourite music to writing music to performing to disdain for Toronto's clique-y music scene.

What Ingrid felt throughout the night was surprise. It wasn't that Ingrid was surprised to be having this conversation with a woman, though, admittedly, at most parties, conversation about music tended to be dominated by men. Nor was she surprised to be talking to a woman — of course she'd talked to lots of women at lots of parties over the years. What surprised Ingrid was that this woman-to-woman conversation never defaulted to talk of shopping or TV or complaints about men.

Also amazing was how Sabine reacted to the things Ingrid said. Ingrid was somewhat shy, felt most comfortable with a guitar strapped to her body or a mike in her face. So when Sabine talked, Ingrid nodded and listened, then suddenly jumped in to agree, to rant, to exclaim. Ingrid had a lot to say, but often waited to say it all at once. And when she did speak, Sabine didn't look at her like she'd grown an extra head or raise her eyebrows in alarm or turn to her neighbour or leave for the washroom and never return. In other words, Sabine didn't act like women acted at parties, didn't hate Ingrid just because Ingrid had expressed an opinion which was outside of the things women were supposed to talk about. Ingrid realized she needed an ally, and here, wonderfully, was Sabine.

'You get this too?' Ingrid asked, now drunk and forthright. 'You tell people you're a musician and —'

'Men think it's cute and women get angry. Angry!'

'I know!'

'They say "Oh I played a little piano years ago."'

'Music is not my *hobby*. I do it, I play, 'cause I *need* to.

'Exactly. And if I didn't want to fuck half the women I meet, I wouldn't even bother with them.'

'Half?'

'The other half of me still likes men.'

'Pardon?'

'Oh don't worry,' said Sabine, looking right into Ingrid's face. 'You're not my type. Too cowgirl.'

'Well, I —' Ingrid felt strangely disappointed, despite never having thought of women in that way.

'And if this conversation's going where I think it's going, well, I have a policy. Never sleep with your drummer. And I can drum.'

Eventually, someone passed Ingrid a guitar, the stereo faded and Ingrid tuned the dirty strings. She tried to pass the guitar to Sabine, who shook her head.

'Piano,' Sabine said.

'What do you know?' Ingrid asked Sabine. 'What can you sing with me?'

'Try me,' Sabine said.

Ingrid played a couple of party favourites: the Tragically Hip, Van Morrison. A small crowd gathered, but she shook her head when someone shouted Bob Dylan, groaned with Sabine at the suggestion she do 'Redemption Song'.

'Tom Waits?' she asked Sabine.

'Yes yes yes,' Sabine said. 'Then one of yours.'

By the end of the party, their throats raw from talking and singing, their bodies full of drink, accompanying each other towards Dundas West, Ingrid and Sabine had formed what would become the Tender Buttons. Not a duo, not Heart.

'And definitely *not* the Indigo Girls,' Ingrid said, weaving with Sabine past gabled houses and paved-over lawns.

'Then what? Who? Meg White and ... not Jack White,' Sabine said.

'Oh, I like Jack.'

'He's very likeable.'

'Meg and Beth Orton?'

'Or Salt-N-Pepa. Luscious Jackson!'

'Old school. All of the above. So, a band. Two women can be a band.'

'Agreed.' Ingrid and Sabine shook on it, at the corner of Dundas and Bathurst, just before Ingrid turned west and Sabine caught the streetcar east.

Jette is the first person Ingrid and Sabine have ever invited to band practice. A week before today, they burned a CD with three of the Tender Buttons' better tracks.

'I didn't listen to it,' Jette explains, sitting on the frayed couch.

'No?' Ingrid frowns at Sabine.

'Just wanted to hear it in person.'

Sabine smiles at Ingrid.

'So what have you got?'

'Well, one of the tracks on the CD —'

'No, Ingrid, something new. Some rough something, a few bars, a few words?'

'I don't usually play anything for Sabine that's not done.'

'Ingrid has a policy,' says Sabine.

'Fuck policies.' Jette grins.

Ingrid sighs, then rummages through her backpack for her notebook, sets it on a music stand and opens her guitar case to tune her guitar. She strums a few opening chords.

'Ugh, E minor.' Sabine rolls her eyes. 'Sad song.'

'Or bittersweet,' Jette adds.

'So far it's called "Rebuild".' Ingrid begins:

> *'You have built some beautiful things*
> *Metal bones and mechanical wings*
> *Kick the city dust from my toes*
> *They are callused, they are worn.*
> *My ankles swell, my feet are burned*
> *Walking walking walking walking*
> *You would sing your need for trails*
> *But your song no longer brings me home.'*

'Needs a chorus,' Ingrid says when she's done.

'You've been listening to some Emmylou Harris. Maybe some Radiohead?' Sabine asks as she sits down at the piano and plays the chords for 'Rebuild'. 'What about changing the G to an F?'

'You and your effing Fs.'

Jette interrupts. 'Reminds me of Libba Cotten's "Freight Train".'

'Of course! Country girl and her obsession with trains.' Sabine pounds out an E minor on the piano. 'Toot toot!' She sighs. 'I'm tired of your tear-in-a-beer songs.'

'Pardon?'

'Lonely girl on a country road loses her man —'

'Did you hear the lyrics? That's not what this is about. I've been trying to write a city song —'

'Okay, lonely girl on Spadina Road loses her man —'

'You're telling me you never wrote a sad song?'

'I'm having a hard time identifying with your lyrics. My parents were immigrants. Maybe I see things differently than you.'

'You were born in Canada.'

'I speak Portuguese at home.'

'You visit your parents twice a year.'

'What about you, Jette? Your parents are Greek.'

Jette looks up, surprised to suddenly be back in the conversation.

'My grandparents. My dad came here when he was four. My parents' Greek is minimal and I know only some scraps. I'm Canadian, with Greek seasoning.'

'And my lyrics?' Ingrid asks. 'Do you have a hard time identifying with them?'

'Uh —' Jette looks at Ingrid, then smiles at Sabine. 'Songs I write, it's not *boys* girls are losing. One of my songs, I played for Sabine the other day and Sabine was like … What did you say, Sabine?'

Ingrid thinks she sees something at that moment, a slight exchange of looks and smiles, a hazy shyness and twinkle in both Sabine's and Jette's eyes. Ingrid bends over her guitar, a pose she often adopts onstage, part stage fright, part concentration, part avoidance, all a need to get back to where she is most comfortable: playing music, singing.

'You mean about the song, right?' Sabine asks Jette. 'What I said about the song? Not about —'

'Sabine, stop,' Ingrid interrupts. 'Look, I was trying to write your big rock song.'

'Sabine and I were talking about rock,' Jette says, 'and what that means. Rock. Cock. Schlock. About a year ago I stopped trying to write "the big rock song".' Jette fingers the quotation marks in the air. 'That doesn't mean that our bands can't rock, but what does that mean? What else can we call it?'

Ingrid retunes her guitar.

'Did you come up with an answer?' she asks.

'I'm thinking we should change the name of the band,' Sabine says.

'What?' Ingrid's hand slips and her guitar strings clang. She pauses while the sound reverberates then fades. 'We came up with it together.'

'Mostly it was your idea.'

'But you liked it!'

'I never loved it. I —'

'I think,' Jette interrupts, getting up and walking to the piano, 'it's all gotta be equal, or pretty soon, some band*mates* start to feel like backup singers.'

Ingrid, her armpits damp, her hands grimy and grey, is already setting up for tonight's gig at Rancho Relaxo when Sabine and Jette finally arrive, together, half an hour late.

'New haircuts? New T-shirts? No invite?' Ingrid uncoils cable on the stage, then stands up straight to retie her ponytail.

'You hate my hairdresser,' Sabine says, approaching the stage.

'I just don't want to look like you. We're not the Spice Girls. What's on the T-shirt?'

Sabine stretches it over her chest, warping the ice cream cone that curls around her small breasts. *Lick Me* is written underneath the cone.

'And Jette got the same one I suppose.'

Near the bar, Jette turns around to show off her *Cunning Stunt* T-shirt. Ingrid groans.

'You're not wearing those tonight.'

'Calm down, jealous Scorpio.'

'Let go, possessive Aries.'

Sabine leaps onto the stage and heads towards the piano, stepping over Ingrid's cables. She sits on the bench and plays a few chords.

'You got it tuned!' she calls towards the sound booth, where the bespectacled technician nods. Sabine turns back to the piano.

'Sabine. Sabine?'

Sabine looks towards Ingrid, scowling.

'Finish setting up. 'Kay?'

'Yes, Your Majesty.'

Ingrid slides off the stage to get water from the bar. She sits beside Jette, who is already halfway through a bottle of beer.

'You smell good,' Jette says.

'I know. I stink. Luckily I have time to shower before —'

'Too bad.'

'What, you're serious?'

'Always.'

Ingrid shakes her head. 'How can you drink beer before a gig? Gas plus nerves plus singing equals disaster.'

'An hour before, I stop. Then afterwards, I gulp back about two pitchers of water.' Jette leans towards Ingrid. Seeming to smell her air, says, 'Then I'll pee for days.' Jette laughs. Despite Ingrid's nerves and her annoyance at Sabine's lateness, Ingrid can't help laughing along with Jette's big cackle.

'Which song we doing for sound check?' Ingrid calls to the stage.

'"Umbabarauma"!' Jette says.

Ingrid looks at Sabine, ready to protest, but Sabine holds up her hands.

'We always do your "Ambulance Siren" song.'

'My song? Isn't it ours?' Ingrid sees Jette smiling beside her, then turns to Sabine and nods.

'"Umbabarauma,"' Ingrid reluctantly agrees.

Post-gig, the trio are standing on College, scanning tiredly for a cab or streetcar.

'I think I'll walk,' says Ingrid, picking up her guitar case. 'Nice night.'

'You heading west?' Jette asks.

'Yeah.'

'I'll walk with you.'

Ingrid turns to say goodbye to Sabine. But the look she sees on Sabine's face — angry, hurt, jealous — keeps her quiet. She smiles; Sabine doesn't. Instead it's Jette who speaks.

'My parents didn't get why I wanted to live in the west end. Like it made me less Greek. But, you know, sometimes you need to get away from your parents, even if it's just the other side of the city.'

Sabine and Ingrid nod knowingly and the tension, the look on Sabine's face, quickly vanishes. They part, and Ingrid wonders if she imagined it.

Though the day and the gig were hot, the air now is surprisingly cool. For once the streets smell fresh and green; there are few invasive whiffs of garbage and sewage. Ingrid is grateful for the cool air on her still-warm arms, can feel the sweat from the gig drying salty on her skin. As they walk, Jette is mostly quiet, but then Jette is usually mostly quiet, as if she gets all the loud out of her onstage. Ingrid doesn't mind. In fact, the quiet is welcome, so different from Sabine. Ingrid processes the night over and over in her head. The missed notes, the off harmonies, reactions from the (pretty good) crowd. Obsessing, Ingrid knows, but a good obsession.

'I'm down here,' Jette suddenly says, nodding towards a side street. Ingrid tightens her grip on her guitar case, about to say goodbye. But Jette is grinning. 'Come with me. I want to show you something.' And Ingrid follows her down the dark, tree-lined street, entranced.

Jette's apartment is in the basement of a house, but it's a good basement — the ceilings aren't too low, the air is fresh, not damp and musty. The main room glows faintly pink from the street light outside the window until Jette turns on lights, disappears into the kitchen and returns with two large glasses of water.

'Sit,' she says.

Ingrid sets her guitar case on the floor and sits on Jette's small, old couch. And that's when she spies the acoustic Takamine, propped on a stand in the corner.

'That's yours?' Ingrid asks.

'Yup. Just don't get it into your head I'm some soft folksinger. You'll ruin my riotgrrrl reputation.' Jette smiles. 'Play something. I've been dying to hear you play it since we met.'

'Really?' Ingrid grabs the guitar. She is impressed by how clean the strings are and, as she strums a chord, by how the instrument is almost in tune. Jette sits beside Ingrid. Ingrid randomly strums.

'Come on, play a song.'

Ingrid's right breast cradles into the waist of the guitar's body. She finds, then tightens a capo on the second fret. She plays a Tender Buttons song and Jette sings along. Then, looking quickly at and away from Jette, she again adjusts the capo, and sings: *'Good night, street light, it's morning.'*

Jette straightens up, surprised.

'What's that?'

'It's my goodbye-Toronto song,' Ingrid says.

'I didn't know you were leaving.'

'It's not Toronto I'm thinking of quitting.'

'What, are you seeing anyone right now?' Jette asks.

'Not really. Thought I'd take a break from boys for a while.'

Jette laughs. 'I hear ya. A good, long while.'

'Well, not forever.'

Since she first met Sabine, and since Sabine revealed she's bi, Ingrid has looked at women quite differently. As if Sabine has showed her a door she hadn't noticed before. Ingrid knows she's not gay. And she's pretty sure she's not bi. She likes boys. Definitely. Sometimes unfortunately. But on the streetcar or walking downtown, whether she's looking at a man or a woman, it suddenly doesn't matter anymore. Sexy, for Ingrid, now transcends sex. So when she finds Jette's fingers stroking her thigh, she wastes no time considering. Ingrid looks at Jette's fingers, then looks at Jette just as Jette leans in to kiss her.

What surprises Ingrid is not that she's kissing a woman, the first woman she's ever kissed like this, with her whole mouth, with her tongue, it's that kissing a woman is not as weird as she thought it would be. In fact, it feels perfectly right. But smoother. No stubble scratching her chin and cheeks. And, when Ingrid reaches towards Jette's chest, wonderfully, there are her breasts.

'This is in the way.' Jette gently removes the guitar and her fingers sweep lightly across the strings; the hum resonates as she starts to unbutton Ingrid's shirt.

'Wait. Wait. I thought you and Sabine...?'

Jette only shakes her head. She pushes Ingrid's bra up and away from her breasts, then lowers her head to run her tongue around her right nipple. Ingrid moans. Men can be all hard. Jette, however, is strong and soft and fearless all at once.

'Oh, Jette ...'

'It gets better,' Jette says. She unzips Ingrid's jeans and yanks off her panties, then kneels in front of the couch. Starting with one hand on each of Ingrid's knees, Jette trails her fingers halfway up Ingrid's thighs, pries her legs open and lowers her own head. Ingrid slides her bum forward, bucks her crotch into Jette's face, her hot breath, then, grabbing chunks of Jette's shaggy hair between her fingers, she pushes Jette's head deep between her legs.

Tender Wasn't the Night with The Tender Buttons

by Misty Taggart

BUCKSHOT DUCK LODGE
with
THE TENDER BUTTONS and THE LEAFY GREENS

at Rancho Relaxo, July 20. Tickets: $5.

ATTENDANCE: 100 / RATING: * * *

With the recent addition of Jette Konstantinos (ex Martian Barn), The Tender Buttons, who now number three, ignited the almost-full but in-flux house last Thursday night. Each woman brought her own sound to the stage — Ingrid Schrader's alt-country, Jette's neo-R&B and Sabine DeSouza's hip-hop-flavoured mezzo-soprano create a unique mash-up of genres that helps the band stand out in a city filled with waif-y, earnest, down-on-the-farm singer-songwriters. Two very memorable moments: DeSouza's crowd-rallying 'Umbabarauma', sung/chanted flawlessly in the original Portuguese, and Schrader's 'Rebuild', which built from delicate piano to swirling guitar towards the triple-harmonized climax: 'There's a danger now in being too good at what you do.'

'Did you read it?!' Ingrid brings the paper to the Tender Buttons' next practice.

'Yeah, we know. We decided not to read it.' Sabine sits at the drum

kit, kicking the bass drum, randomly punctuating the conversation. *Boom.*
Boom.

'We? Why?'

''Cause a review takes you outside what you're doing,' Jette says.
Boom.

Ingrid nods and looks at Jette, who hasn't looked at Ingrid since she
arrived. She folds the entertainment rag and puts it back in her guitar case.
Boom. 'Sabine, quit it.'

'You're cranky. That time of the month?' Sabine asks.

'Who's cranky? Sabine, it was a good review. If you —'

'No, you. It was good for *you*. Not for us.'

Jette looks up from her guitar, eyes wide.

'You said you didn't read it.'

Boom. Boom. Boom.

'Maybe I glanced at it,' Sabine says.

'The article mentions *two* highlights, "Rebuild" and "Umbaba —"'
Ingrid starts.

'"Umbabarauma" is Jorge Ben's song, not mine.'

'You make it yours,' says Jette.

Sabine groans and rolls her eyes.

'Sabine helps make it ours,' Ingrid adds.

'Lay off the sentiment. I'm getting tooth decay.'

Jette's arms suddenly fly into the air, then land back in her lap.

'Look, my guess is you wanted me here not just to sing but to give
you some advice. Right?' She looks at Ingrid, then at Sabine; they both
nod. 'Good. Great. Don't read the reviews. Don't fight over whose lyrics
are whose, whose name goes first, whose song gets sung at sound check.
It's a collective, a band, not a bunch of individuals. Fucking put that ego
and angst into writing and playing songs or you'll never move forward.
Ever.'

Ingrid looks at Sabine. Sabine nods at Ingrid.

'Okay, well, speaking of writing songs,' Ingrid starts slowly, 'Jette and I
were talking.'

'You were? When?' asks Sabine.

Ingrid hesitates, then says, 'Thursday night. Jette's got some experience with recording and —'

'You talked about all this, just on your walk home?'

'More or less,' Jette says.

'More or less what? Walk? Or talk?'

'Sabine. Focus.' Ingrid's heart is thumping but she tries to talk calmly. 'I just think we need someone else to record our stuff. When we try, Sabine, we end up bickering.'

'That's why we have Jette.'

'We didn't get Jette to be our ref.'

'I'm right here, you know,' says Jette.

'Okay, Jette, what do you think?' Ingrid asks.

'We tried recording our own stuff with Martian Barn. The results weren't bad, but yeah, we'd squabble so much that the process was too slow. You want to spend weeks and weeks arguing over a couple of lyrics or notes, do it yourself. You want the process to be faster, get someone else.'

'Okay,' says Sabine. 'So we get someone else.'

'We can't afford anyone else. We made forty-eight bucks at the Rancho Relaxo gig.'

'Fine,' Sabine says. She looks at Jette. 'But you being more than a singer, you recording us — well, it'll change things.'

'I'm open' — Jette grins, looking at Ingrid for the first time — 'to change.'

'What do you think of the recorder?' Ingrid and Jette are rolling westbound on the streetcar, post-practice.

'The kiddie instrument?' Jette thinks. 'Not much range.'

'But what if that's exactly what you want?'

'I don't get it.'

'Let's start over. Look. The CN Tower. What do you see?'

'I see' — Jette leans over and looks out the window — 'a phallic symbol.'

'Everyone says that. What else?'

'It's a magnetic needle pointing south. Guides the Bay Street suits to their money.'

'When I was a kid I'd come to Toronto with my parents. Three-hour drive. By hour one I couldn't stop looking out the car window, waiting for it. Somewhere outside Mississauga, there it was, shimmering in the heat, the tallest thing around. I swore to my parents that when I grew up I'd live in the city so I could see it every day.'

'Now you live here and there it is.'

'But how often do I look at it?'

'It's not the Eiffel Tower.'

'No, but it's fucking huge and I ignore it. So does everyone. Last time I was up it I wasn't even ten. Tourists come here for a week and see more of the city than we do in a year. Why do I pay so much rent to live and work and play in this tiny section of the city — no bigger than the small town I grew up in?'

'And the recorder?'

'It's the first instrument I ever learned. That song I played the other night? It's kinda about saying goodbye to an older Toronto, feeling as dizzy as the Sam the Record Man sign, treasure-hunting in Honest Ed's, a ride on the subway like a roller coaster, paid for with magic tokens. Now Sam's shut down and Honest Ed is dead. So with this new song, I want to use instruments like the recorder —'

'To get that innocent sound.'

'Yeah, exactly! Ooh, goosebumps, shaky knees.' Ingrid presses her palms onto her knees. Jette puts her hand on Ingrid's. Ingrid moves their hands closer to her crotch. A man standing above them looks quickly at their hands, then away. Two women, so what? Ingrid thinks. An urge fills her, the same feeling she gets onstage when a gig is going well: to yell, to rebel, to kick at anyone who ever said she couldn't. She leans in and kisses Jette, tongue and all.

'I really want to, you know,' Jette finally says. 'Record you.'

'Us. You mean the band.'

'Right. The band. If Sabine can relax. If not, well, don't let anything stop you. You have some great ideas.'

'Any*thing* or any*one*?'

'The merry threesome,' Sabine says when she arrives at the practice space. 'Let's make a merry noise!'

Jette is setting up equipment — computer, mikes — and Ingrid is helping.

'Late as usual,' Ingrid says.

'I —' Sabine begins, but Jette interrupts.

'First rule: no bickering. Or I'm outta here.'

Sabine dramatically puts a hand to her mouth, then sits at the drum kit and adjusts the cymbal stand.

'Let's start with "Menina Má",' says Jette. '"Bad Girl".' She grins as she translates.

'This is one of my favourites of yours,' Ingrid says to Sabine.

'The Tender Buttons'. Not mine. Right?'

'Right. Okay.'

'Hey,' Jette says. 'Don't break the first rule already.'

Sabine begins: *'You tell me to be good / Give me one good reason / I can be as sweet as the sugar you crave.'*

When the song is finished, Jette clicks a few things on her computer, then says, 'I've always liked the lyrics, Sabine, but sometimes I think … Those angry chords, that sort of smashing quality to the song — I wonder if you should tone it down.'

Ingrid cringes.

'Tone it down?' Sabine repeats. 'This from a woman named Jette.'

'Sabine, Jette's heard a lot of music. Give her a chance to explain. Her opinion's not out there.'

'You want it to sound more like a good girly-girl Ingrid song?'

'No,' Jette says, sighing. 'I don't want you to take the energy out of it. Just pull back on some of the effects. You've got a wall-of-sound thing happening. But careful that wall isn't impenetrable. More piano, less drums. You play such beautiful piano. I don't think Ingrid' — Ingrid opens her eyes wide and shakes her head to get Jette to stop — 'is all girly-girl. Ingrid, why don't you try that "goodbye" song you played for me?'

Ingrid wants to crawl inside the back of the piano. Out of the corner of her eye she can see Sabine's nostrils flaring.

'Okay. What's going on here? Seriously. Ingrid, what "goodbye" song? When did Jette hear this song?'

'After the Rancho Relaxo gig,' Jette says. 'I invited —'

'I thought …' Sabine stops. She so rarely stops, Ingrid finds the sudden quiet jarring. Finally, Sabine calmly says, 'I thought you agreed with the policy, Ingrid.'

'Remember Jette's advice,' Ingrid tries to joke. 'Fuck policies.' She smiles. Sabine doesn't. Instead, she looks at Ingrid, then at Jette, then back at Ingrid.

'What else does Jette fuck?' Sabine asks Ingrid.

Ingrid's first thought is to deny. Deny, and change the subject. But before she can speak, before she even opens her mouth, Jette speeds past her.

'So what, 'Jette says. 'So what if we fucked. So fucking what. It shouldn't matter. We're here to make music, not fucking bicker about mine and yours, songs or otherwise.'

Sabine stands up from the drum kit, then sits back down. Grabs the drumsticks, then drops them on the snare drum with a rattling clatter. The three women listen as the noise fades to silence. Sabine's quiet unsettles Ingrid. She flexes and twists and bites her fingers, desperate for them to be moving. Doing something. She looks at Jette, who's been focused on her computer. Finally, she looks at Sabine, who is staring straight at her.

'I knew this would happen,' Sabine finally says. 'Three women. It's an unholy trinity.'

Jette snorts, then closes her laptop with a slap.

'I'm gonna take a walk,' she says, though she is packing up her equipment, her microphones, her cables, putting it all with her laptop in her backpack. Sabine and Ingrid watch Jette. Hear the zipper on her backpack. At the door, Jette looks back at both of them.

'Call me,' she says to no one in particular. She leaves.

Ingrid stares at the closed door for a few beats. Finally, she turns to Sabine.

'I think you just got dumped.' Sabine smirks.

'It's not like we were —' Ingrid stops and gulps. 'It was just twice.'

Sabine shrugs. 'Whatever.'

'Really? Just, whatever? I thought you liked Jette.'

'Sure I did. But that didn't stop you, did it?'

'You can't claim her, Sabine. It's like what Jette said. About our songs. It won't work if we keep tabs. Keep declaring what's mine and what's yours. We've gotta share.'

'So I can have her now? Gee, thanks. If I fucked a guy you liked, there's no way you'd be okay with sharing.'

'That's not what I meant.'

'Maybe that's the problem. If we knew what was mine and what was yours, you wouldn't have crossed those bounds.'

'Oh come off it. You can't say a person is yours. What I mean by sharing is we gotta work with her, together. If we want to record —'

'Jette's going back on the road with Martian Barn in October.'

'Seriously? Why didn't either of you tell me?'

'Seems there's a lot we weren't telling each other,' Sabine says.

Ingrid begins to pack up her stuff — her guitar in its case, her notebook in her backpack.

'So we're done here?' Sabine asks.

Ingrid snaps the clasps on the guitar case.

'What more is there to say? We keep talking, we're gonna start sounding like catty women at parties, jealous over shopping for T-shirts.'

'This is so much more than T-shirts, Ingrid. Or do you think it's not 'cause we're all women. 'Cause there's no guy around to make this seem more serious.'

Ingrid gets up and goes to the door of the practice space. She turns once more to Sabine.

'It was just, whatever. Fun. I didn't think about it too seriously.'

'Obviously.'

'Could say the same about you and the music,' Ingrid says as she leaves.

All week, Ingrid tries to call Sabine but all week Sabine keeps her phone turned off. Ingrid decides to drop in. Hopping on the eastbound streetcar, Ingrid wonders if this is one of their problems. The west/east divide. The streetcar crosses over Yonge and the view out the window changes from office buildings to churches to sari shops. West versus east. Once people settle in the city, they don't switch sides.

Sabine lives in a top-floor bachelor, part of a house that's mutated into several small apartments — periodic hot water, sloping floors, thin walls. Sweltering in the summer, a view of the lake in the winter. With each step to the third floor, Ingrid rehearses her opening refrain, her chorus. Her heart pounds like it does before a gig. A feeling she's used to, which gives her courage. She finds the door with the jingle bells and knocks. Ingrid hears scrambling, stomping, swearing.

'Sabine?'

'Just a sec!' The door swings open. 'Was doing the dishes.' Sabine stares at Ingrid, then disappears back into her apartment. Ingrid leans her head over the threshold and sees Sabine half buried in the fridge. She emerges with two bottles of beer.

'Been saving these.' Sabine motions to the kitchen table, which is crammed into a corner under the low, sloping ceiling. Ingrid closes the door and enters, ducking to sit. She looks at the label before Sabine pops off the cap.

'*Weizen,*' Ingrid says.

'*Ruhet in Frieden,*' Sabine says in German.

'The rest is peace.' They clink bottles.

'So.'

'So.'

Ingrid drinks, and swallows. 'I guess I didn't get it. How you could like men and women. I didn't see it beyond a phase,' she says.

'Now you know? That it's not a phase?' Sabine asks.

'Yeah. Except for me. I'm pretty sure it was a phase. With boys, well, it's easier to figure out what they want. They're not so subtle.'

Ingrid and Sabine laugh.

'Depends on what you want,' Sabine says.

Ingrid picks at the label on her bottle. 'Like the band. Why were we doing this? To be famous? To have fun? To write and perform songs?'

'Depends on what you mean by famous. A review on *Pitchfork*? Getting played on CIUT? The CBC? Commercial radio? As long as it's still fun.' Sabine drinks her beer.

'As long as we're still writing. Together.' Ingrid peels her label clean off her bottle. 'Ah-ha!' she exclaims, and hands it to Sabine. She smiles. Sabine rolls the label into a tube.

'So...?'

'So, Sabine, looks like we have different ideas of fun. Banging your drummer versus banging the drums.'

They pause.

'*Estou com saudade, não triste,*' Sabine says in Portuguese.

'What's that mean?'

'My mom says it to me when I'm leaving her house. *Saudade* is kinda non-translatable. It's missing someone, but knowing that you can't go back to the way things were. I am feeling *saudade,* but I am not sad.'

'Good. 'Cause, well, I'm gonna record my stuff. My songs. And —'

'With Jette.'

'Well, that's the thing. How can I? She's leaving, and being friends with you is more important to me than she is. So I'm gonna do it on my own. Get a line of credit, get advice. And the person whose advice I really want, really need, is you.'

Sabine smiles.

'So we *will* still be friends,' she says.

Ingrid laughs.

'Absolutely,' she says.

CD RELEASE

INGRID SCHRADER

with special guests HIGH NOON

Thursday, February 11
@ The Cameron House, 408 Queen Street West

'There's someone here I have to thank before this last song. Sabine DeSouza? Where are you?' Ingrid hears a squeal as Sabine jumps to her feet. She is wearing a silvery dress that sparkles as she twirls. From the stage Ingrid squints into the shadowy audience. 'Sabine was there for me throughout so much of the recording of this album. When I said glockenspiel, Sabine said marimba. When I said harmonica, she told me to whistle. Thank you, thank you, thank your sweet heart, Sabine!'

There are cheers and wolf whistles from the audience. Ingrid strums her guitar as she waits for the audience to hush.

'Sabine, since you're already dressed for the occasion, would you mind coming up here to help me with a song?' Sabine does not hesitate. The audience hoots and applauds as she climbs the stairs to the stage. Ingrid grabs an extra mike that's been waiting behind a curtain. The women stand side by side, centre stage.

'Sabine is all over this album —' Ingrid begins.

'Like a smear,' Sabine interrupts.

'— but this was the last song we recorded together.' There are boisterous sobs and sniffles from the audience.

'One last hurrah for the Tender Buttons,' Sabine says. 'So I get, what, five percent of album sales?'

'That's right, a nickel of every dollar from sales goes right into Sabine's glittery pockets.' Ingrid leans away from the mike and towards Sabine. 'Thank you, Sabine.'

'Congratulations,' Sabine replies.

Ingrid strums the first notes of 'Good Night, Street Light', and Sabine closes her eyes. Begins to sing:

> *'You're like a sailor's sunrise*
> *Bleeding day from black to grey*
> *Cool welcome your forgotten light*
> *Where were you all night?*
> *I know you'll leave, the sun will set*
> *Good night, street light, it's morning.'*

At the end of the song, Ingrid and Sabine bow and curtsy. Sabine leans over and gives Ingrid a hug. Ingrid's guitar keeps their bodies from touching.

Mona Says Fire, Fire, Fire

November came in like a lion and is leaving like a pride, tearing at its kill. As Mona Berlo stacks her wood, throwing it into a wind so strong that the wood might slingshot back, she is bracing herself for Refugee Cove's fall into winter by committing to a life by fire. Before, heat, like love, was convenient and temporary, a switch on the wall when needed. Now, maturity and experience tell her that both are work, are muscle-and-body rewards.

Since moving from megacity to Refugee Cove, Mona wakes up most mornings not surprised by where she is but by how easily she's been able to fill the corners of this new life, as if someone pressed a button, clicked a mouse and here she was. Clicked a moose, as they say here. So teaching French at the district school fits into her plan, like weight loss. Her friends, those city mice, married and childrened, divorced or approaching, have a heaviness about them Mona doesn't want to gain. The combined mass of debt, relationships, family and careers, with the added carbon and diesel in the air, is suffocating.

To better her French, she enrolled in a six-week French immersion program in Trois Églises, Québec, the summer before she moved to Nova Scotia. She and dozens of randy teens stumbled off the train at three in the morning ready to party, not study. Mona bonded quickly and necessarily with anyone close to her age and by the end of the first weekend, she and MBA candidate Jeff Hassani were the first to acquire nicknames: Monsieur D'Argent et Grand-mère.

After a week, the fervour was as contagious as strep throat in a co-ed dorm. They found themselves dizzily dancing to separatist hip hop, drunk on bottled Expor', bumping hips on the sweaty Friday-night dance floor beside fellow students almost half their age. And then, unable to go back to the rooms in their billeted houses, they found the lee side of a woodpile in a dewy-grassed backyard. They broke the French-only rule when neither knew the word for condom.

'I was stacking my firewood today and thought of you,' Mona now says into the phone. She laughs slightly, then stops. 'I'm finding myself thinking about you. I talk to you in my head. I've done long distance before. A few hours away, weekend visits. But a time zone? I want to be a grown-up. Love letters and sad phone calls seem very first-year university. Very French immersion.'

'Breakups and honeymoons,' Jeff says.

'Midnight sun then weeks of darkness.'

'Have you ever seen the northern lights?'

'From the plane, last time I saw you.'

'They don't just look beautiful, Mona. They *crackle*.'

'Do you have a minute, Madsozwelle Berlo?'

Colin's dad. No time for parent-teacher time. Mona hesitates before saying, 'Of course.'

'Well, Colin? He's a bit upset about French. He — his mom wanted' — he pauses, his mouth shifting on his words like a horse's chewing a sugar cube — 'if there'd been some last year ...' He shakes his head. 'Keeps getting harder,' he says.

'Yes.' Mona nods, though she doesn't know if he means school, or parenting, or life. Mona pretends he means teaching, and this helps her nod. Nodding calms her — the bobbing, a raft in the sun. Avoiding his eyes, she stares at his Fundy Bay Tractors cap, which, she guesses, is hiding a receding hairline.

In Québec, when Mona kept struggling with the language — oh, how she wanted to stab Dr and Mrs Van der Tramp so hard in the face! — Jeff soothed her. He said that the only way to learn a language was to dive into the water and hold your breath for as long as you could, until you emerged with gills. But the second trick, the secret trick, is to get past the point of panic, to get to the peace that comes before drowning. She wants to relate this now to Colin's dad but Mona has noticed in the community a habit of male ease, of keeping boys boys for as long as possible, before they have to give in to their lives of labour. The girls do better in, or care more about school. They'll need it in the future. Most of these boys think they won't. Once on the water, their survival suits will save them. If they wear them.

'Don't worry, Mr Gillin. He'll be parlez-vooing in no time.' *Vive la révolution!*

'Call me Rubin.'

Rubin. Yummy.

'Then call me Mona.'

'Moona,' he pronounces.

On the winding road from town, the birches bow towards each driver like commoners greeting a queen in her procession. The setting sun has escaped from a week of clouds, gilding the last yellow tamaracks. Mona would stop her truck, pull over, take a picture, if she wasn't already stalled on the gravel shoulder. Waiting for the kindness of a stranger isn't what worries Mona, nor is abandoning her nineteen-year-old, $900 4x4. It's the wildlife: she's seen more moose and deer on this highway than traffic. There have been rumours of cougars.

Just when Mona sees through her tears that it's fully night, the high beams of a large vehicle fill her truck. She stays in the driver's seat until Rubin's moon face is in her night window.

'We were heading back from the Santa Claus parade.'

'We?'

'Me and Colin.'

'Santa already.' Mona climbs into Rubin's truck. Colin is sitting behind the passenger seat like an early Christmas present, wrapped bulkily and tied with a scarf, blond hair wind-licked. Mona turns to greet him but he tucks his head into his coat. Students can't handle teachers outside the classroom walls, these unpredictable, in-the-wild collisions as terrifying as a husband and wife meeting his mistress at the grocery store. Fight or flight. Rubin revs the engine and they drive away.

'I've been waiting for this to happen,' Mona says of her truck.

'Good I came along.' Rubin says *good* like *lewd.* 'Answering the call, large or small.'

'Of nature?'

'No.' Rubin laughs. She hears Colin laugh too. 'I'm a firefighter. I volunteer.'

'Oh.' Mona pictures Rubin swinging her over his shoulder like a bag of bait.

They drive in quiet for a time, then, rounding another corner, Rubin swerves away from a raccoon, who, in the road, pauses, stunned in the headlights.

'What was it, Dad?'

'An elephant.'

'Wasn't big enough!'

'Willabee wallabee we …' Rubin stops singing and looks at Mona. 'I hit a deer once and thought a lady in a fur coat had fallen from the sky.'

'Do you hunt?'

'My dad took me out when I was a bit older than Colin. But death's death —'

'Dad?'

'Yeah, kiddo?'

'Can we go?'

'Hunting? You get some older, Uncle Teddy'll take you —'

'Really?'

'Sure, Bud. And when you get a big buck, Teddy can show you how to string him up, dig a knife into his belly, pull out his steaming, wriggling guts —'

'Daa-aad!'

'Never cared to hunt after that,' he says to Mona. 'Not a popular opinion around here.'

'But you fish?'

'I fish,' Rubin responds flatly, just as they begin their descent into the village, where the trees open up and the wide bay unfurls before them. A crescent moon hangs low above the water, turning the heaving, breathing bay into liquid metal. It's something else that amazes Mona — how much light even this sliver of moon can cast when there is no other light in the sky.

As they drive along the main road, the only way in and out of Refugee Cove, Mona counts infrastructure: hospital, old folks' home, older folks' home, store, post office, library, fire hall, school. What more does anyone need?

A health-food store, an independent cinema, a gastropub. Mona chuckles softly. Rubin looks at her but she shakes her head.

At Mona's rented house, Rubin gives Mona the name of a cousin, or cousin's cousin, who'll pick up and fix up her truck for cheap. He helps bring in her groceries, refusing her offer of beer or money for gas.

'Big house for one girl.'

Woman. 'Keeps warm.'

'Cold now. You don't have a furnace?'

'Just the wood stove.'

'Sure you won't freeze?'

To death? 'It's a good stove.'

Living alone in the big house, Mona dresses and undresses wherever she is, spreading her discarded clothes from room to room, shedding pieces to inhabit the many spaces. So on the kitchen floor, by Rubin's foot, is one sock and a pair of red-and-white striped panties. Little sailors. Her eyes look away quickly but not quick enough, and Rubin follows her glance to the floor, to the panties. Too late; he has spied them like a fox sees a rabbit, and Mona holds her breath and closes her eyes, the rabbit frozen in the second before the chase.

'Get your fire going,' Rubin says as he leaves.

'You know anything about fixin' trucks? Mine's right fucked,' Mona says to Jeff after she describes her day.

'You're sounding like a local.'

'Well, shit, who'd'a thunk?'

'I know the subway schedule. I've changed oil. But seriously? Sadly, I have to get going. I'm checking out this Detroit band at the Horseshoe. I'll call later. After. Promise.'

'The horseshoe above my door blew down last week. Is that good or bad luck?'

'Now *that* I could fix for you.'

'The 'shoe or my luck? Okay, pack up your Robertson and move out here. The locals would be relieved I have a man around.'

Jeff pauses.

'Do you think about my moving there? I'm crazy about you, I'm grad-uating this year —'

'I don't know.'

'What don't you know?'

'Whether we're too old to be crazy or too crazy to be old.'

The bells ring out for Sunday. Mona hears them blearily through her dreams. She can see the white wooden church through her bedroom window, the simple tin lightning-rod steeple poking into a grey sky. At breakfasts earlier in the fall, when it was still warm enough to open her windows, she could also hear the choir's faint hymns as her porridge slapped to a boil.

In the Maritimes, these small churches belie the size of God. The opposite of Québec, where vigorous black devil-horses built silver, multi-steepled mountains — rocket ships to heaven. Now, as the number of parishioners dwindles, they are as empty and cold as Mona's house, through which she tiptoes, moving thinly between the few remaining warm molecules. Waking to the realization that Jeff didn't call (as promised) is like finding her Christmas-morning living room unvisited. No gifts waiting under a blinking tree, stockings hanging too lightly by a dead hearth.

When she calls Jeff and he doesn't answer, her worry for him turns to anger as she scrambles eggs, hints at hatred as she chews, then shifts back to worry, for herself, as she stares through her frosted front-door window at the low-tide harbour. She runs upstairs, untying her housecoat, reaching for long johns. Tide's out; get out.

Mona flaps in her rubber boots through the bar harbour — the enormous bowl of empty sea mud that suctions her down, past her ankles. The landscape could be Mars, as red and uninhabited, but with gravity increased, pace heavy and reaching. Buried clams spit water through air holes as she passes. She spits back.

The wind has become several winds, swooping together and apart like seagulls. She begins to hear the mewl of an ATV advancing towards her. Wreck-reational vehicle. The back-punching wind cannot push her home fast enough, and quickly Rubin pulls a four-wheeler parallel.

'Need a lift?'

'No, I —'

'Come on.'

'I hate these, you know.' Mona kicks a wheel.

'Not mine.' He revs the engine. 'Hate makes you weak.'

'Have an extra helmet?'

Rubin removes his and Mona pulls it over her toque. To see she has to keep her head up, point her eyes at the sky. It smells of Rubin's sweat, a dirtier salt than the sea air, and is warm from his breathing. She climbs onto the back of the beast, legs split wide.

'Hold on.'

'Where?' There are no extra grips.

'Love handles, Mona.'

The engine snarls so she can't protest when Rubin turns away from her house and up onto the beach. The four-wheeler settles bumpily into other tire ruts, and she grasps Rubin's waist firmly.

There are exceptions to rules; Plan B's are mapped along with Plan A's. Mona's Plan A — move east, reduce costs — was not only monetary but personal. Six months earlier Mona had grown tired of the chase, catch, and release of relationships. Purging her belongings began a cleanse, a fast from the past. Returning to the land, breath by fresh breath, was to be a return to herself.

Then, in Québec, she met Jeff Hassani.

Damn. She has fallen in love. Yes. Yes she has.

His not calling and her anticipation otherwise has embarrassed her. She begins to feel dangerous, and has an urge, holding onto Rubin's waist, to bite the exposed skin of his neck, to open the wings of her pelvis into his lower back, to ride this machine like a teenaged girlfriend. Even through their thick fall clothes, she feels hints of a fusing of bone, a salt flavour she has missed but now craves in her taste buds.

'You wanna see something?' Rubin asks.

'I do.'

Rubin turns abruptly onto a hunting path that leads into the surrounding cape. Two-week-old snow lingers in ditches. Wind diminished, Mona's ears and fingers begin to tingle and hum as they thaw.

Rubin points. Up ahead Mona sees crimson splattered and soaking into the dirt and gleaming on the rocks.

'Fresh,' Rubin says. He is talking about the kill sight — moose or deer. But Mona lightens her cling from his waist.

Eventually they reach a cleared place — only birches lean in lonely clumps among stumps of former evergreens. She can see the bay through these trees, so they have come to the other side of the cape. Rubin stops the four-wheeler and the sudden quiet seems louder than the vehicle.

'What is this?'

'There's a squatter's shack down on the beach. The guy died about a month ago and the kids have taken over.' As proof, Rubin kicks a beer can with his rubber-boot toe.

'Did he clear-cut this whole area?'

'Paper towels. He just cut a path.'

Mona decides to stop buying paper towels.

At the bottom of a roped-off, slickened path is the low-tide beach of Kettle Cove, where, in the water, beyond the arena slope of tens of thousands of smooth, round rocks, sits a large, bowler-hat island.

'No one home,' Rubin says.

'On the island?'

'No.' He smiles. 'There,' and he tilts his head towards the cabin, the tiny home as tight and neat as a seashell. She begins to bend and collect rose-and-white stones, their muted glow like buds in the gravel.

Rubin has marched ahead.

'We'll check out that shack,' he declares.

'Actually.' Mona stands straight and looks around. The sky and sea are the same slate grey, the island deep brown. Aren't Jeff's eyes that colour? 'I'm cold.' Her fingers have stopped humming.

'You're cold.' Rubin's voice fills with rejection. 'Come on. You're no fun.'

'You sound like Colin.'

Rubin tilts his head; his neck muscles tense. She knows this pose from Québec: the pause, the wait for comprehension. Rubin needs a moment to understand the sounds that form his son's name.

'He gets it from somewhere.' His face darkens as he begrudgingly tramps back in the direction of the four-wheeler. Mona drops extra rocks from her hands and trots after his giant steps, pebbles in her pockets tinkling, a tiny echo of the retreating waves as they shift and disperse the shore.

Rubin doesn't say much on the ride back to her house, though he didn't say much before — the motor was too loud. But he is driving more slowly now, and Mona holds on to the edges of her seat. She wonders if his neck was that red before.

Rubin slows at Mona's door and she removes the helmet. He revs the engine but Mona shouts, 'Wait!' He cuts the power.

'Here.' Mona pulls an oval rock from her pocket — a large, dull pearl, white with a ribbon of pink wrapping its circumference. Mona quickly adds, 'For Colin. He's studying rocks and minerals.'

'Seems he studies rocks and minerals every year. All we are is rocks and minerals.'

'And fossils,' Mona adds.

'Stilbite.' Rubin pockets the rock, turns the vehicle away from Mona and double-toots his horn. He zips off and she waves to the back of his neck.

When Jeff finally calls close to midnight, he talks immediately and rapidly, rushing through apologies and explanations like a teacher squeezing out the last words of a pre-recess lesson: too late to call last night, up early and away this morning, no answer this afternoon, busy, busy, busy —

'Mona?'

'You woke me up.'

'I miss you. I've been dying to talk to you all day. Don't fall asleep. Five more minutes. Three. Please.'

Mona doesn't want to believe his explanations.

'Okay, okay. I'll let you go.'

'Let me go. Seriously. I can't figure out the use of "us" right now.'

'What do you mean?'

Like he's a lick of flame, she snuffs him out.

'I can't do this right now. Us. We aren't an us, and until we can be, what's the use of us?'

Mona has fallen asleep with the cordless phone in her hand. The ringing wakes her again.

'Mona Mona Mona.'

'Who is this?'

'What d'you mean "whose this"? "Whose is this?"' The voice mocks at a higher pitch.

Rubin. Drunk Rubin.

'Whater yer doon?'

'Sleeping. I'm working tomorrow.' She should just hang up but she doesn't know what will make things worse.

'I want my tongue yer little pebble.'

Worse.

'I have to go.'

'Emergency! Emergency! Did I wake you? Sleep then, go to sleep.' He hangs up. Mona's sleep deepens with the sounds of her phone: dial tone; frantic, off-the-hook bleating; silence.

* * *

Rubin's on the deck of the red. One by one the boats are returning, managing the high-tide channel below the leafless, smudged cape. Through tonight's rare calm, Mona can hear their motors as she watches the parade from her living room window. She learned quickly whose cousins, dads, uncles and brothers worked on which boats and whose grandfathers first owned them. She can guess which boys in her class will eventually fish and which girls will raise their children. The boats are toy-shaped, broadly crescent-bowed and flat-sterned. Green and grey and orange — crayon versions of the landscape. The last one is the colour of steamed lobster. The faraway men, their legs triangular for balance, are bending, passing, coiling and packing, readying for a quick dock, a fast exit in the eight-cylinder trucks that cost twice, sometimes three times as much as their houses. Mona decides that's Rubin at the stern of the red boat, tossing scraps of bait to the swarm of gulls. She wonders about his smell, stronger than the sweat in his helmet: salt and rubber and metal and herring lingering on the hands and arms that look twice their size on his abridged body.

No one is tall. Height is for the city, its limited space. Here men grow wide and strong to fill the distance.

After sunset, she is counting cars in Rubin's driveway. Her excuse is Colin's week-long absence.

Rubin's truck is there, his wife's van is not.

For a moment Mona watches Rubin through the open kitchen door. He is sitting by a wood stove in an oversized, worn brown armchair, reading the paper, bottle of beer by his woollen toe. He looks showered and fed. A log snaps in the stove and Rubin glances over at the stove, then, slowly, at Mona.

'You here for supper?' He folds the paper.

'No, I —'

'Come in, then. Don't take off your shoes.'

'Homework.'

'Not done, Miss. Lobster ate it. They'll eat anything — other lobsters, drowned bodies. Sit. Coffee? Beer?'

'No, no. I just —'

'Rum.' Rubin gets up.

'Lots of Coke and water.'

Rubin pours two.

Mona sits at the kitchen table. The room smells like smoke and boiled pasta, the sweet smell of baby powder and used diapers under the tidied, piled clutter.

'What was for supper?'

'Batch pasta. Tawna took the baby to her mom's. They go when I'm fish*en*.' He hands over the glass. 'Here's to heat.'

'*À votre santé,*' Mona replies. 'I brought some work for Colin. Where's he?'

'He's in Moncton till the weekend. His mom'll be away at Christmas. Guess someone should have called but that's responsible parenting. Why start now? Will he miss much? Sometimes a week with his mom's better than school, you know? Sometimes.'

'*His* mom? So Tawna isn't his mom?'

'Tawna isn't. I was seventeen when we had him. Didn't care, too stupid. You get pregnant, you only think about having the kid. What else would you do here? Babies is one of our industries. Have a kid — save the school! Why I'm fishing and why he's a shithead. But then you could say that about most of us. The homework' — Rubin gets up and holds out his hand — 'he will do this weekend.' He takes the papers, then throws another log on the fire.

'When you get off the boat, I mean, when you step onto the dock after a day on the water —'

'Or a week.'

'Okay, or a week. How do you feel at first?' Mona sips and waits.

'Landsick. Did you know when there's an earthquake, land moves like waves?'

'I taught that in science.'

'Not just a drunk ol' dad.'

Mona sees her pebble then, her Sunday gift, lying on a small table beside the brown chair. Rubin follows her eyes, then grabs the pebble and hides it in his hand.

'Ah,' he says. 'Captured.' He rolls it like a coin over his fingers and knuckles and suddenly pops it into his mouth. 'I ate rocks when I was a kid,' he says, the pebble clacking behind his teeth. 'Wish you had been my teacher. Maybe would've stuck with school.' He spits the pebble into his hands, then drops it back on the table. His saliva has darkened the pink middle to red.

Mona gets up and stands beside Rubin. She bends and reaches over his knees, grabbing the rock. She can see Rubin's teeth in her periphery, white and wet, peeking around his open lips. The fire behind her is making the backs of her legs sweat. She tilts and, losing balance, twists and straddles, her left leg around his knee. Rubin's hands, on his lap, twitch just below her crotch. She straightens, then plops the pebble into her glass of rum. Tiny drops splash onto her neck, his thumb and knee.

'I want this back,' she says, sitting down. 'To show the class.'

'Show and tell.' Rubin speaks slowly, and leans forward, moaning her name. '*Moh*na.'

'Fire,' Mona says, eyes wide, pointing. 'Fire, fire!' She jumps up.

Papers are flaming, as is Rubin's sweater, which he is wearing. In seconds, Rubin has the sweater off, wrapped and extinguished, and has shoved the papers into the stove.

'Colin's homework. Jesus.' Rubin breathes.

'You're okay.'

'Okay. Stupid. Stupid.' He checks his arm. His T-shirt has a smudge of char. Nothing more. 'Stupid. Fuck.'

'How's that sweater?'

'No need for mouth-to-mouth.'

'No mouth.'

'Neck-to-neck, then. Shoulder-to-shoulder.' Rubin opens the kitchen door, letting in air and out smoke. He hangs his sweater on the railing.

There is a crackle then, outside the wood stove, a fierce static that turns into words: *Attention all firemen, attention all firemen, please proceed to the fire station. You have a fire at thirty-seven-oh-two highway one-oh-eight. All units required to respond immediately to —*

Rubin lunges for the two-way radio on top of his fridge.

'Holy shit, this is a real one. That's the old Higgins place. That crazy broad's burned it down. We always said … Come on, come on, fuck! Let's try and get to the station. First one there gets the truck!'

They just miss the fire truck. Mona drives to the Higgins place so Rubin can get changed beside her, though she's driven standard as many times as there are gears. Mona forces her concentration onto the highway and away from glimpses of skin, of muscle, of hair. The truck pitches, sputters and hiccups around each turn.

Smoke blacker than the night sky. Heat that penetrates the cab of the truck. Mona could turn off her headlights. Men are running around, shouting. Mona lets Rubin out, then parks the truck. She stands on the shoulder, watching, arms crossed. The Higgins place, the large, white century home that loomed like an iceberg at this sharp turn in the highway, is now just flame and smoke. Though the firemen have hooked up their water truck, it is as useful as a garden hose. Rubin pats another man on the back.

'Hot one,' Rubin says as he drives them back to Refugee Cove. 'Went to school with their oldest kid. Before we got there he was trying to run in and save his track trophies. Not that you should, but what one thing would you wanna save?'

'I got rid of most of my stuff before I moved here.'

'There must be one thing you still got. One thing you love.'

Mona thinks.

'Jeff Hassani.'

'How's that?'

'No. Yes. My partner. I have a ... boyfriend. Had. Have, I guess, still.'

'You sure?'

'I'm starting to be.'

'Me too. The fires do that. Just wanna go home and kiss my kids. Go over our escape routes. Stop drinking and burning.' Rubin pulls up beside Mona's house and looks at her. 'Just bored flirting, mostly. Now it's over. You teach my kid so let's not be weird. It's too small here to be weird.'

'Well look at us. Being right adult.' Mona grins.

'Surprised?'

'I'm starting not to be.'

'Go call your man.'

'Thanks for the ride.'

Mona makes Moncton in time to see the metal bird's descent from the sky. Around her, friends and family chirp and sway, eyes fixed on one set of doors, the one with the sign that reads BIENVENUE! WELCOME!

She sees him. He is taller than everyone else.

'*Bienvenue!* Welcome!'

The rain has stopped for the dark drive back. She expects something around each corner, and then there he is, in the middle of the road, legs splayed, lowered head and antlers as big as the front of the truck.

'Don't honk,' Jeff whispers.

'Hell no.'

The moose regards the truck as if it were a leaf. He sniffs the ground, then turns, slowly walks into the woods and disappears. Mona breathes and drives on.

'It's a sign,' Jeff says.

'It needs a sign. Moose crossing.'

They come to the ruins of the Higgins house and Mona pulls over.

'And what was the cause?'

'Ashes in a cardboard box. Something everyone's done. One hot coal.'

Jeff rolls down his window.

'So dark and quiet. I can smell ice and trees and wood smoke.'

Mona gets out of the truck, runs over to the passenger side, leans in the window and kisses Jeff.

'That moose will be there if you leave here. Blocking your way.'

'I'll stay if I can start your fire,' Jeff says.

'Je suis chaude.'

'J'ai chaud,' Jeff corrects. *'"Je suis"* means you're horny.'

'Exactement.'

Some Just Ski and Shoot

Nadine grabbed two suitcases and some garbage bags. In twenty minutes she had packed most of her clothes. Though she hoped she was leaving for just the weekend, that Ian would call and beg her back, she knew it would be longer. As Ian watched TV, Nadine began to steal the *theirs* and *his* of six years of stuff, moving fast, heart thumping, as though the apartment were burning. Art books. Jazz CDs. Photographs both framed and loose. A concert T-shirt. Letters. Camera. Finished, she slouched and panted at the bedroom door. Closing her eyes, she wanted to memorize Ian. She knew that even after she left he would continue to breathe, his hair and fingernails would keep growing as on a dead body. He lay, gathered and calm, buoyed by pillows.

'I'll get my furniture soon. I'll email. Don't fuck her in my bed.'

Ian rolled his eyes. 'The couch is mine.'

'The couch is yours. Fuck her on the couch. Please don't kill my plants.'

'I won't.'

'Really? For some reason I don't trust you.' Nadine heard the cab honk. She heaved together her bags. Ian didn't offer to help and Nadine didn't know if she wanted him to. 'I won't be one of those girls who keeps calling. I won't write you two years from now hoping there's still a chance.'

'I know you won't.' He nodded, eyes on the TV.

Nadine's own eyes strained against tears. She looked a last time into their bedroom. Ian was pale and still, fading.

Predictably, the train to Sarnia stopped dead between two flat fields, the three-hour trip well past hour four. It was February, but it was also southwestern Ontario — winter was months of November until spring. No twists in the land to stop the sharp, fast winds; no snow to lift and soften the frozen, stumbling mud. As this view darkened to indigo, mist rose near the edges of the woodlots and hovered. Nadine's face began to reflect in the window, steadily clearer. For a while, she watched herself chew her fingernails, the overhead lights erasing her eyes. She held her cell phone in her lap the whole time, checking often to make sure it was on, that the ringer was loud enough; she changed *ring* to *vibrate*. She perused the list of names and phone numbers and stopped on *Us*. She changed *Us* to *Ian,* then deleted the number.

The train reached Sarnia two hours later, and, as Nadine stepped onto the platform, the wind tore into her lungs, freezing her inside out. Even in the cold she could smell Sarnia: rotten eggs and rubber. Waiting in the station was Candace, her cheeks as pink as her scarf, her face as excited as a long-distance lover's. They hugged. Nadine was always surprised at the soft smallness of women's bodies, their yield and touch, round places to hide. When Nadine hugged Ian, he rarely bent to meet her. She had to stand on her toes, straining, his body an abrupt resist. Nadine and Candace were level. If Nadine stood on tiptoe, she could rest her head on Candace's crown. A year ago, while hugging her goodbye at St. George Station, she had kissed her cheek near her lips. Down, not stubble. Candace had blinked and pulled away, then smiled and jumped onto the chiming subway. Now, seeing Candace again, Nadine felt her stomach muscles warmly twisting, even though the parking lot air was dusty and headache-cold.

'There's the car.' Candace bustled away to unlock her car, her corduroy legs whipping. She threw Nadine's suitcases into the trunk, then leaned in to move them aside for the other bags. Her cords sat low on her hips, her jacket rose up, and Nadine spied Candace's tattoo, the Chinese characters gooseflesh on her back above her red underwear.

'I always loved your tattoo.'

Candace yanked at her jacket.

'*Zi you,*' she pronounced. 'My tramp stamp. I regret it. I got it right after high school.'

'Free,' Nadine translated. 'Don't regret anything.'

'Even Ian, then.'

'That'll take time.'

'Coffee?'

'After that let's go to the waterworks.'

'No boats or fries in February. Too cold for couples.'

'Lots of blank sky and lake. We'll keep each other warm.'

At the water-filtration plant, Candace and Nadine sipped their coffee. The car windows began to steam.

'Remember Todd?' Nadine asked.

'You messed around in high school.'

'I lost my virginity here two days after the New Year's party you and Wayne threw. Coulda been romantic but it was cold and it hurt and one of the things I kept focusing on was the foul taste of coffee in his mouth, like vomit. Reality edits romance.'

'I try not to think about that party. I lost my virginity in the bandshell at Canatara Beach.'

'That was with Wayne, right?'

Candace cracked her window. Waves slapped against the breakers.

'Um, actually, no. I was at a party one July and met this older guy and we drove there and it happened. I was fourteen — summer before high school. I never saw the guy again — he was from outta town. We didn't even use a condom. Stupid. I can't really remember his name. I never told anyone 'cause I was kinda embarrassed.'

'I can't believe you never said.'

'Old secrets have an expiration date. We shouldn't stay too late. I have to work tomorrow.'

'I don't want to go yet.'

Nadine sat up straighter, moving closer to Candace, the fingers of her left hand gripping the edge of her seat. She wished impossibly for anything to keep them there a little longer, some distraction, and shifted again, trying to get close to Candace without looking like she was trying. Candace kept her eyes on the water.

'Don't,' she said.

'What?'

'Kissing me wouldn't be a good idea.'

'I wasn't —'

'You look ready to pounce.'

'Why can't I kiss you?'

'Rebound, rebound,' Candace chanted like a foghorn.

'I'm not thinking rebound. Just fun.'

Candace shook her head as she started her car and blasted the defrost. Her face was suddenly ghoulish in the dim dashboard light. The Fort

Gratiot lighthouse beamed green into the car, sliding the light over their faces, then back out across the black lake.

'Are you seeing someone?' Nadine asked as the car backed up.

'That's not the point.'

'Then what is the point?'

Candace straightened the car and stepped on the gas.

'Nadine, you can't now think you're going to be a dyke 'cause you got dumped by another guy and men aren't working for you. That's not how it works.'

'A woman can sleep with another woman and not be a dyke. Sex is sex. Didn't *you* say that everyone's bi?'

'That was before I realized I was gay. Maybe you do need to fuck someone but it's not going to be me.' Candace shifted and drove away.

As Candace parked in Nadine's parents' driveway, Nadine shuffled around for her scarf and mittens, and said, 'I wish someone kept records.'

'What are you talking about?' Candace replied.

'Well, in the history of Nadine and Ian, he'll always be the dumper and I'll always be the dumped. I hate this right now. I want to puke, having to walk into my parents' house. I was thinking on the train about how I knew.'

'You always know. Everything is trying to warn you. You can smell it in the air. The water tastes off.'

'The water always tastes different in Sarnia.'

'Okay, so here you know when things start smelling and tasting *good*.'

'Yeah, I mean, I'd started applying to out-of-town schools, was trying to save money. I'd even donated a sweater he'd given me. It wasn't a bad sweater, it just didn't fit right, and the fact that it didn't fit bugged me so much I couldn't wear it. How many times were his hands on my body?'

'How many times, then, was he thinking of your body while he was *in* your body?'

'I was already ending it and Ian could tell. He just beat me to it. Jerk.' Nadine climbed out of the car and got her bags from the trunk.

'Try to sleep,' Candace said just before Nadine closed the car door.

'We'll see,' Nadine answered. After Candace had sped down the sleepy street, Nadine wished she'd made some plan to see her again. Soon. Without a plan, her nausea broke into empty loneliness as she opened her parents' unlocked door.

* * *

Because her parents wouldn't let her see her boyfriend, in her second-last year of high school Candace had moved out of their house and in with Wayne. Their apartment was just behind the school, so Nadine went over often to do homework, smoke Wayne's cigarettes, choke back his canned beer.

When Wayne started going to Western, Nadine sometimes slept over. Candace said she missed his breathing, missed the cycle of their paired sleep, as if in the night everything quietly fit and traded: skin and legs and hair confused in dream. Candace said she would wake up and forget where she was and who she was, that each night her and Wayne's selves were becoming not just each other but a new other, like mating and keeping the genes. At seventeen, still a virgin, Nadine didn't completely understand, though she wanted to. Nadine had just started to date Wayne's friend Todd, and envied Candace's apartment, the inside privacy, its tease of adulthood. Talking late, Nadine would fall asleep in Candace's bed instead of on the couch. The longer Wayne was at school, the smaller the sleeping space between the girls became. They wrote on each other's backs, tracing large, upper-case letters, pressing hard when someone guessed *A* instead of *H*. One morning, Nadine awoke curved backwards into Candace's body, Candace's bare thighs stacked against her bum, her left arm wrapped and skimming her nipples, her breasts pressed flat against Nadine's shoulder blades. Needing to pee, Nadine didn't move until she heard Candace yawn, felt her sniff her neck.

'I like how you smell in the morning,' Candace said, rolling onto her back.

'When I sleep here, I always think I smell like you.' Nadine also rolled onto her back and reached under the covers to pinch Candace's thigh. Candace grabbed her hand and spliced her fingers between Nadine's, then rolled onto her side and pressed her face into Nadine's neck. Nadine wrapped her legs tightly around Candace's thigh. Nadine could feel Candace deeply breathing, feel her body's oxygen pulled into Candace's lungs. Candace kissed her then, her mouth soft yet hard, her tongue dry. When she stopped, Nadine's lungs emptied and she gasped.

'I have to pee,' Nadine whispered.

'Me too.' Candace released Nadine's hand and got out of bed. Nadine watched her tread barefoot down the hall, straight to the bathroom at the opposite end, in a Western T-shirt and flowered underwear.

She sat on the toilet, the bathroom door open, and rolled her underwear to her knees.

Now I'm tired, Nadine thought. The women were downtown at Ups and Downs, Sarnia's only pub. All week, sleep had been the idea of sleep: lie in bed, eyes open. She watched her life form in the shadows of her old bedroom, along the rows of tiny pink rosebuds that for twenty years had lined her walls. Jail-cell bars, she'd once thought. She tried to rearrange those shadows, her back to the clock that counted the hours like minutes. And when she thought she had it arranged, her ideas vanished, all guesswork anyway.

'Now I'm tired,' Nadine said to Candace as she sat down with two fresh pints. 'I can't sleep when I should and I dream when I'm awake. I'm glad you called. How much for the pints?'

'My treat.'

'God, when was the last time I heard that?'

'Six years ago?'

'Thereabouts. I had my first bar drink here on St. Patrick's Day, in grade twelve. I got a margarita 'cause it was green. I figured I could handle the tequila 'cause I'd had a shot at your place on that New Year's, but I'll never handle tequila.' Nadine paused. 'I'm sorry about the other night. We don't have to talk about sex and stuff. I mean, not togeth — I mean —'

Candace smiled. Nadine relaxed.

'Don't worry about it. And don't forget we're friends.'

'You forget about friends when you date someone for a long time. I could have worked on that more.'

'Everyone could work on that more. You also forget to be friends with your partner. My last few relationships ended and I realized we hadn't even been friends in the first place. So what was I doing with them? I'm sure we could all remain friends a lot more often if we were friends to begin with, or used that as the foundation, not sex.'

'Not *just* sex.'

'Friendship and sex. That's a better marriage.'

'How long has it been —'

'Almost a year.'

'What happened?'

'I guess we both wanted serious but a different kind of serious. You know, being queer can be friggen tough, but sometimes I like that I can't fit into whatever people want women to fit into. I *liked* that marriage wasn't an option. Then when gay marriage was legalized, Brooke got really excited and I didn't. Brooke said I was too angry. I said she was too naïve, and, well, you know how it goes. Let me ask you something,' Candace added. 'Can you name a sexy, middle-aged, married dyke?'

'Outside of Hollywood? Not that I know —'

'Exactly.' Candace sat back and crossed her arms. 'Out of gay men, hets, and dykes, dykes are having the least amount of sex. So many dykes I meet want desperately to be in a committed relationship. They find someone, drive a moving van to their second date, stop having sex, gain all this weight, buy a house and become the fridge and stove.'

'I guess 'cause so many girls start planning their weddings in high school, or, actually, before high school.'

'I had other things to figure out in high school,' Candace said.

After Wayne came home for the winter holidays, Nadine didn't see much of Candace that last Christmas of high school. She also didn't see much of Todd since he'd taken some extra holiday shifts at work, and therefore wouldn't be able to make Candace and Wayne's New Year's party. Nadine didn't really mind.

The only plans she had for New Year's were to have fun, drink (not too much), dance, spend time with Candace. She would not think of her legs, of her hands, of kissing her lips, of their shared, hot breath. Candace was her friend. A *girl* friend.

Wayne had invited a lot of his friends to the party. Some had come from London and had been staying in the apartment for a couple of days. Candace introduced Nadine ('my best friend!') to most of them. Nadine, watching Candace, forgot many of their names, except dyed-orange-haired Trisha, who watched Candace just as attentively as Nadine did.

At midnight everyone cheered. Candace and Wayne kissed against the wall, tongues sloppy. A couple of Wayne's friends asked Nadine for a New Year's kiss, and at first she obliged, thinking them sweet, until one guy pressed his beer-stinking mouth against hers too hard and moaned.

An hour into the new year, Nadine stumbled towards the bathroom. For the first time that night she didn't have to wait in line. As she opened the door, she hoped there was still toilet paper. On the edge of the bathtub was Candace, her sweater and bra pushed over her breasts, tinsel hanging between them, her jeans and underwear bunched at her ankles. Trisha was kneeling, her back to Nadine, Candace's red fingernails in her orange hair, her head nodding between Candace's legs. Candace opened her eyes, saw Nadine, then closed them, and, with one hand, waved Nadine out of the bathroom.

Nadine did not close the door tightly. Her legs felt as tight and hot as her face. She shook her head and heard Candace command:

'Faster, Trisha. Don't stop!'

Nadine found Wayne downing another can of Blue in the kitchen.

'Hey, you didn't hear it from me, but Trisha is eating out your girlfriend in the bathroom.'

Wayne snorted.

'Yeah, right.'

'Go join 'em.' One of his friends laughed.

Wayne looked at Nadine, her face pale.

'You're fucking serious.' He put his can on the counter; it dropped to the floor, beer spilling and fizzing as he bolted to the bathroom.

'You fucking dykes!' Wayne shouted. Everyone in the apartment turned.

Two days later, at the waterworks, in the back of Todd's dad's car, Nadine finally let Todd fuck her. He began with his fingers, the nails chewed and jagged, then, quickly, when he realized he could, unzipped his fly, pulled out his dick and shoved it, forcing, until it was inside. He came abruptly; Nadine didn't. His body was heavy and her legs cramped. Though it did hurt like she knew it would, she was crying before the pain.

Nadine never revealed that it was she who had told Wayne. After the party Wayne and Candace broke up, and word spread quickly that Candace was gay.

'I would have liked to have figured it out on my own,' she had told Nadine.

'You were well on your way.'

'I still wasn't ready to tell myself, let alone the whole town.'

Candace tried to move back in with her parents, but they had heard the news and wouldn't let her come home. She could barely afford the apartment alone. She had to start another part-time job and her grades slipped.

Though not as often, Nadine still came over. Now she brought groceries and movies, as well as homework.

'Nadine, you don't have to.'

'I feel like I have to.'

'You trying to be my girlfriend?' Candace smiled.

Nadine coughed.

'No. I mean, I *am* your friend.' And Nadine swore to herself that, from then on, she would only think of Candace as a friend.

When high school ended, they both went away to university — Nadine to Toronto, Candace to Montreal. They called, they wrote, they visited, at first making contact almost daily, then weekly, then a few times a year. Relationships came and went. For a couple of months Nadine dated a woman.

Candace had been living in Sarnia again for almost a year when Nadine and Ian broke up. After Candace's father died, her mother became very sick, and despite years of tension, Candace moved back, to help. Nadine admired this, doubting she'd ever do the same.

Now, at Ups and Downs, Nadine was glad she was too tired to get drunk. She found herself watching everything she said.

'Do you bump into many people?' she asked. They'd both kept turning towards the door.

'Not too much, and I'm a bit surprised. I guess people have actually moved on, or have kids and homes to hide in. I think I saw Todd one day. If it was him, he's lost a lot of hair.'

'Coulda been. It was thinning in high school. I think he stuck around and got a job at the plants.'

'Give him a call,' Candace suggested. Nadine tried not to feel slapped by it, brushed off.

'No thanks. Fucking him in high school was one thing. God, the losers we put up with for dick. Or used to.' She looked at Candace. 'Nowadays, I don't think I'd consider him a, uh, whole lover. I mean you finally meet a couple of decathletes, and after that, with some others, I'd rather download porn and masturbate.'

Candace nodded.

'Male or female, there are a lot of triathletes out there.'

'And some just ski and shoot.'

As they cackled, the men in the bar turned to stare, then shifted in their booths and on their stools.

'I *am* glad you're here, Nadine,' Candace said. Nadine felt Candace's foot brush against hers.

'Good, I was worried.'

'So how was Ian?'

'I guess I kidded myself that it was good. There was enough other stuff, besides sex, going on. I've been thinking, hey, I didn't come that much, he didn't pay much attention to me. Or change positions. Guys hit thirty and lots of them, like Ian, can only ski. You try not to fall asleep, waiting. Do women know more what they're doing?'

'Not always. Some don't know what makes them or their partners come. Can't communicate it. Same athletes, different games.' Candace thought for a moment. 'Or same games, different uniforms.'

'And how are you?' Nadine blurted.

'I've done my training.'

Nadine pushed her foot harder into Candace's. Candace slowly moved hers away.

'I already said we shouldn't.'

'Why?'

'We're friends.'

'So? Great.'

Candace was quiet a long time. She finished her beer.

'I'm not gonna be a rebound.'

'You're not —'

'Nadine, I can tell right now that I will be. I've been wondering if this going out tonight was a good idea. Maybe not. Let's take a bit more time, okay?'

'What do you mean?' Nadine tried not to think that the conversation sounded like another breakup. Candace stood and put on her coat.

'You have to relax,' she said. 'You have to heal on your own.'

After a week of trying not to, Nadine had to call Candace.

'What do you want?' she asked.

You, Nadine thought. *Your unchanged body. Help.*

'I didn't want to ask —'

'Ask what?'

'Well, I have to get my stuff. Ian just left a message. He's moving out of our — his — *the* apartment. My stuff's still there. I have till the end of the month. I'm gonna get movers —'

'You can't do it alone.'

Nadine started to cry and Candace was quiet.

'When do you wanna go?' she finally asked.

They took Candace's car and Nadine paid for gas. On the 402, Nadine suddenly realized how unknown Candace now was, how presumptuous she'd been to expect anything from her based on one kiss almost fifteen years ago. They talked like acquaintances, getting to know each other during the three-hour drive. Nadine watched the landscape, so much garbage in the ditches, broken stalks of corn, skyward explosions of starlings from naked woodlots.

Nadine got very quiet as they neared her neighbourhood. She marvelled at how everything kept moving — snow had fallen, had been shovelled, and had melted, garbage was still collected, mail delivered. Robins had begun to return.

'He won't be there,' Candace said.

'What will?'

They struggled up the stairs, arms full of empty boxes. Nadine's heart banged as she unlocked the door.

It was like coming back from vacation to a robbery, though nothing had been stolen. The air felt smoky and invaded, like a magician had just disappeared. This was not her oxygen. All her furniture said nothing — it ignored Nadine, or seemed to have been replaced by duplicates. Maybe she had expected her hanging clothes to reach out and hug her but the shirts were motionless in the closet. Then she looked towards the bed — the last place she had seen Ian.

'Candace! That's not my bed.' Nadine started shaking. She lifted away a new duvet.

'Where *is* your bed?'

'That's a good question.'

Nadine stomped about. Opened every cupboard and closet.

'It's here, in the hall closet. Disassembled.' She relaxed.

'Do you think outta guilt he bought a new bed?'

'I guess. I told him not to fuck her in my bed, though that didn't stop him while we were still together.'

'Bad vibes, then. Couldn't get it up in your bed. Let's pack.'

'Then leave this haunted house.'

While Candace was direct and thorough, Nadine was scattered — spending five minutes in the bedroom, twenty sitting on his couch, staring. Candace took a break and joined her.

'A couple weeks before,' Nadine started, 'we had come home from a movie and were sitting here on the couch, talking. We used to joke about weddings and all those clichéd couple things, I guess to prove we weren't like that. When we started dating I was twenty-four and was thinking more about jobs and sex, not my wedding and kids. So the first few times Ian and I talked, I let him know that marriage wasn't on my mind, and he never said anything about it, never agreed or disagreed. He passed the test. Then a few months ago he turned to me on this couch and suddenly stated, "You don't want to get married," only realizing that after six years together. I always thought he didn't want to either. After *living together,* we weren't able to communicate anything. And then, knowing that I was losing him, and control, I started to stumble and say "Sure I do, just not now, I mean, maybe ..." I was *negotiating* for something I didn't want. For what? To not be alone? If I'd convinced him, and we'd gotten married ...' Nadine paused and looked at Candace. 'I'm sorry, it's hard to concentrate.'

'Don't worry about it.'

Nadine got up and packed the bathroom, then Candace double-checked.

'You forgot some brushes and gel. And your hair dryer.'

'Those are Ian's.'

'So Ian wanted to be the prettiest one in the relationship. Now the breakup makes sense!' Candace laughed, and eventually Nadine laughed too.

'Hey, did you want to keep any photos?' Candace asked.

'Not anymore.'

Candace tossed a handful into the garbage.

After a few hours Nadine's stuff was sealed in boxes, and their hands were black from newspaper.

'I gotta wash my hands. Ian said he'll be back late, after eight, so we have a bit of time before we should get to my aunt's.' Nadine went to the washroom and ran water in the sink. Candace came in and stood behind her. 'Thank you so much for helping.'

'How do you feel?'

'Good, actually.' The suds turned grey in her hands. 'I keep thinking he's getting off too easily. I wish I could do something to his shit. Smash his computer, set fire to his bed —'

'There's something *we* could do.'

'What do you mean?'

Candace moved beside Nadine. She grabbed the soap and Nadine's fingers between her own hands, everything slippery in lather.

'Let's dirty his sheets.'

'We shouldn't have washed our hands.'

'We should for where they're going.'

'Ah.'

During the time Ian and Nadine lived together, the only large possession he ever bought for them, not just for him, was the couch. Never towels or sheets, rarely groceries. He'd hated doing laundry and making the bed. Ian's new sheets on his new bed were masculine navy blue.

Nadine drove Candace's car to her aunt's. They hadn't really spoken since they had carefully remade Ian's bed, covering their salty stains, their pine-and-earth smells soaking into the sheets and pillows. Nadine was still smirking as they hit the highway, where Candace removed her right hand from the steering wheel to suck herself off Nadine's fingers.

'You said that wasn't going to happen.' Nadine and Candace were sitting on the front steps of the old apartment the next morning, waiting for the movers, the weather undecided between sun and snow. They sat close to keep warm, their breath clouding as they spoke.

'It was a special occasion,' Candace said. 'Have you thought about what you'll do now?'

'For the first time in years it feels like I have no attachments. My stuff's packed and will be stored, Ian's gone. I should really feel clear but I'm still sad and I feel guilty for being sad.'

'When my dad died my mom and I packed his stuff a month or so later and it was terrible. Once the boxes, full of all that solid stuff, were sealed and gone or stored, I felt like I was finally free, closing up my body too, making it solid again. Then my heart and thoughts slowly followed. When you love someone, your heart splits your body open and when that love suddenly ends, it takes a while for your body to recover. There are things that are always there, and regrets, and the memories from a smell or an angle of sun. The end of anything big is significant, it's all like the end of a life. You have to mourn that life you thought you had. Use it to move on to the next one.'

'Around you I always felt like I was learning.' Nadine paused. 'I want you but don't want to need you.'

'Then it's time to live differently.'

The moving van screeched up and parked in front of the apartment. Nadine directed the men, then stepped out of the way and watched as her boxes and furniture were effortlessly carried downstairs and loaded. Six years moved in less than an hour. After the van was gone, Candace left to get her car. Nadine sighed, her mind as empty as the old apartment, her body reassembling.

Happy Meat

They met in the city. Anders had been hired to help build the lofts above the art supply store where Leah worked the cash. They dated off and on for almost six months, until one night, as Leah was closing up and cashing out, the store was robbed by two teens with a sawed-off shotgun. After taking everything from the register, they filled their backpacks with money from the safe, then hit her on the side of the head with the butt of the gun. When she woke up at the hospital, Anders was sitting at the foot of her bed.

'Well I'm sick of the city,' he said. 'How about you?'

They moved to Nova Scotia because farmland was cheap. They sold everything except essentials, and with his EI and her disability, plus savings and donations from parents, they had enough to put a down payment on sixty acres of unseen pasture, garden, woodlot, orchard, stream, barn and house, though it would take the summer and a CMHC mortgage loan before they could live there. They loaded up Anders's compact pickup, and set out on May Day; two days later they hit the Maritimes, where every other house was for sale or abandoned.

'Something tells me we're going in the wrong direction,' said Leah.

'Less competition when the sea levels rise,' Anders replied.

The first night on their land it was warm enough to sleep outside, so they camped under a maple beside their barn.

'This is our tree,' Anders said, gesturing at the branches of the old maple.

'This is our dirt,' Leah said, digging her hands into the dark soil. Anders sat beside Leah on her sleeping bag and lifted off her T-shirt. She lifted off his. They lay down under their tree and slid off their shorts. Their hands found each other's as they looked through the branches at the stars beyond.

'Where to start?' Anders wondered as his hands felt the goosebumps on Leah's thighs. Leah sat up then, and, straddling him, lowered her body onto his. 'Whoa,' Anders said, grabbing Leah's waist and lifting her slightly off him. 'What about a condom?' Leah shook her head and closed her eyes.

'Start here,' she whispered into his ear.

That first summer and into autumn, Leah and Anders slept in the loft in the barn and cooked over an open fire. Construction and farming weren't new to them — Anders had crewed on house and condo projects, and Leah had moved to Israel at nineteen to live on a kibbutz. They worked sixteen-hour, sunrise-to-sunset days, clearing and tilling land for a market garden, renovating the old farmhouse, harvesting the woodlot for firewood and tending to the cow and two dozen chickens they'd bought for dairy, eggs and meat. As the garden grew, so did Leah.

Anders finished the downstairs of the house just as the air turned from crisp to frigid.

'Good,' said Leah, after she'd canned her last bean and pickled her last beet. 'Next year, we'll need help.' And with that, Leah flopped down beside the wood stove into a faded red chair, closed her eyes and slept. Anders knelt beside her, placed his ear on her belly and said to the kicking baby, 'I can't wait to meet you.'

The baby was born in the house with a midwife in February and they named him Timothy, after the grass that grew taller than Leah in August, when she had first felt him kick. A week later, a laying hen and two meat birds were killed by what Anders thought was a coyote, so he reinforced the coops and bought a rifle from a neighbour.

After Anders put their name on the WWOOF website, the volunteers began to arrive in May. They came from out West, from Ontario, from California, Québec, Maine, the UK, Germany, Australia, even South Africa. They came in small groups or in couples or on their own. Some stayed for a week and did more work than others would do in a month. They pitched tents or slept in the barn. Most of them were in their early twenties and vegan-thin, their clothes faded and stained and frayed, their hair matted or braided or shaved or twisted into dreadlocks. They brought guitars and helped with supper and wanted their English corrected or wanted to know everything about organic farming. Others barely spoke, and scowled at the baby whenever Leah had him nearby. They mostly worked with Anders, picking endless weeds, mending fences, sowing seeds, harvesting early vegetables, gathering eggs, milking the cow; some helped Leah at the market.

'Now we know there's another world out there,' Anders said one night to lighten Leah's mood. 'Other than farming and babies and white faces and red necks.'

'This is all the world we need,' she replied.

The WWOOFers came and went. When Leah and Anders found themselves alone on the farm, Leah put Timothy in a basket under an umbrella and worked beside Anders in the fields. They barely talked while they worked, and at sunset they'd go back to the house, scrape food into their mouths and collapse together into what Leah called the family bed. Instead of having the sex he wanted, Anders listened to the quick, animal breathing of his son, the baby a chasm between him and his lover, and counted how many weeks it had been. When he touched her, Leah laughed and said she was still sore. That she was bleeding. Always her breasts were too tender, the baby finally asleep, Anders too sweaty or pushy. Once he suggested they ask a WWOOFer to babysit, just for an hour.

'Are you kidding?' she said, Timothy clamped as usual to her breast. 'And what if something happens?'

Leah's breasts. Oh how they'd grown. At night as she slept he watched them rise and fall with her breathing as he stroked himself under the sheets. He became jealous of his son who squawked every time one was taken out of his mouth. Hadn't he once, while she nursed, heard her moan with pleasure? Oh, oh, Leah's breasts.

'Do you always have to nurse in front of everyone?' Anders had just crawled into bed beside Timothy and Leah after drinking whisky and smoking pot by the campfire with their latest WWOOFers, two lads from Ireland.

'Are you serious?' Leah propped herself up on an elbow to stare at Anders. 'What do you want me to do, go hide behind the corn every time Timothy cries?'

'No, it's just, maybe people of different cultures —'

'They're from *Ireland*. They probably have long-lost relatives all over the Maritimes. I don't get how North Americans go by the millions to see snuff films but think breastfeeding is disgusting.' She paused and fingered

Timothy's toes, which even in his sleep made his face screw up and wrinkle like an old man's.

'They're not your tits anymore, Anders. They're his. And when he wants them, he gets them.'

'I love your breasts. They're part of you. You're not flattered that I look?'

'If you want to stare at some breasts, go feed the chickens.'

The Irish lads, it turned out, were gay. Anders found them in the barn loft the next morning, curled into each other like spoons. They could have been doing it for warmth, but their embrace was more intimate than anything Leah and he had shared in months. He quickly left the barn and started up the chainsaw. Today they would chop and stack wood.

Heidi and Graham arrived the last week of July. From BC, they had been WWOOFing across the country since April. Anders and Leah's farm was to be their last stop in Canada before heading south. They reminded Anders of himself and Leah when they had first started dating. He did some quick counting and realized with surprise that that was less than three years ago. Watching Heidi and Graham work, how quick and sure and tanned they were, how they teased and touched each other often, made Anders feel like an old man, and he wasn't even thirty. Anders scratched his scruffy beard and showed Graham how to milk the cow.

By the end of the first day, Anders and Leah agreed that they had really made a connection with Heidi and Graham. It was actually the first thing he and Leah had agreed upon in a couple of weeks. The second day, Heidi and Graham had drifted into old-fashioned gender camps — Heidi helped Leah with the garden and meals and baby, and Graham helped Anders in the woodlot and fields. At night they ate around the fire by the barn. Anders pulled out his guitar, the first time he had that season, and rolled a couple of joints. Even Leah, who Anders rarely saw without Timothy in her arms, put him on a blanket and accepted the joint when it was passed her way. The scowl and worry that had lined her forehead, the sadness in her eyes, faded away and she talked once again about art and school and farming and the city. She laid her hand on Anders's thigh, then her head on his shoulder. He ran his fingers through her hair, which looked black in the firelight. She had let it grow since moving to the farm. After

Heidi and Graham went to bed, Leah stayed beside Anders until the fire died down and she drifted to sleep.

'She says she doesn't want kids. That'll change.'

It was after dinner the next night. Anders was reading about apple orchards and Leah was knitting mittens.

'Graham told me they might adopt some day. But not till after they've travelled.'

'I think it's selfish,' said Leah.

'To travel?'

'To not have kids.'

'What could be more selfish than having kids?'

Leah stopped and glared at him.

'What do you mean?' she asked slowly.

Anders closed his book.

'The world's reaching its carrying capacity but people still feel they need to go forth and multiply. It's like matching your couch to the wallpaper — you want your own kids 'cause someone else's won't look like you. Sure those kids aren't your flesh and blood, but sometimes the matching couch has a broken spring.'

'Are you saying you didn't want Timothy?'

'No, that's not it at all.'

'You want to know why it's not selfish?' Leah asked. 'Think natural selection. People who grow their own food, who don't clear-cut the land, who hang their clothes to dry, sell their TVs, are the very people who should be having children.'

'Leah says you have a gun?' Graham asked Anders as they were clearing alders from the woodlot.

'What else did she say about it?' Anders hacked a branch, then threw it on the pile.

'I was asking about people hunting around here and she said kinda quietly that you have a gun, to talk to you, and she turned around and went back to the house. She's not too happy about it, I gather.'

Anders stopped cutting branches and wiped his forehead.

'Before we moved here she was held up at the store where we worked.'

'Jesus, was she shot?'

'No. No. Thankfully. Hit, not shot.'

'So why do you have it?'

'Bought it last winter from an old guy down the road. So far I've only shot a rabbit. Two years ago I woulda never thought I'd own a gun, but now fresh meat tastes happier after a winter of turnips and frozen chicken.'

'I've never even held a gun.'

'You can do more than hold it.'

Graham followed Anders into the basement where he kept the gun and bullets. Leah was in the kitchen when they came back upstairs.

'Oh shit,' she said when she saw the gun.

'Graham asked —'

'I shouldn't have mentioned it.'

'Sorry, Leah,' Graham said.

Leah kicked the red chair, then sat heavily in it.

'Here.' Anders handed Graham the rifle. 'I'll meet you by the barn.'

Graham nodded and left.

'Leah.' Anders knelt beside the red chair. 'Leah, it's part of life here. It's a way to get food —'

'Bullshit. It's a way to kill and scare, like all fucking guns. You try having one shoved in your fucking face.'

'Leah.' Anders leaned closer and put his hands on her arms.

'Don't touch me,' she spat.

Anders stood up.

'Is this the problem? You won't fuck me 'cause I have a gun in the house? You gotta get over it, Leah.'

'I was over it until you got the gun. Get over it? What you need to get over is your fucking obsession with sex. There are more important things to worry about.'

'Not for us there isn't.'

'Don't have kids,' Anders said, taking the gun from Graham. 'They ruin your sex life.'

'They can if you aren't open to other options,' Graham replied.

'No.' Anders shook his head. He raised the gun and sighted a crow in the cornfield. 'No. I couldn't discuss that with her.' He took a bullet from his pocket, loaded it into the gun and returned it to Graham. 'It wouldn't work.'

'What, being flexible? Sure it can.' Graham aimed the gun at the crow. 'Can I shoot it?'

'Wait a sec.' Anders stood behind Graham and guided his hands over the gun onto the right place.

'You're flirting.' Graham laughed. Anders blinked, dropped his hands from Graham's, then laughed too.

'Just fire the gun,' Anders said, plugging his ears.

'It's the second time this week I saw that dog,' said Heidi. The two couples were talking farming and drinking whisky around the fire. 'I thought it was a coyote but it's blacker and has different ears. Floppier.'

'Anders wants to kill it,' said Leah.

'You get chicken, Timothy gets milk — it's all part of the food chain. Last winter when I was breaking their necks you didn't mind.'

'Sure I mind. It's why I was a vegetarian for years.'

'You'd kill a dog?' Heidi asked. 'Jeez, Anders, just when we were starting to like you.' Heidi grinned at Anders. Anders caught her look, noticed that Leah didn't, then stole another glance at Heidi's bare legs as she crossed and uncrossed them.

Anders, emboldened by the whisky, reached under the bedsheets for Leah's hip.

'Cool it, Anders.'

'Well, fuck, how long has it been?'

'I'm not counting.'

'Two months? Three?'

'Good night, Anders.'

'I'm gonna jerk off.'

'Just don't shake the bed. It wakes me up.'

'Fuck.' Anders threw back the covers and jumped out of bed. Timothy began to fuss.

'Great, Anders, great. I was just dozing off.'

'Well I'm wide awake,' he said, pulling on his jeans. Leah sat and picked up Timothy, placing her right breast in his mouth. Anders sat on the bed and scowled. He reached out for Leah's exposed left breast, but she moved away.

'What do you want?' she asked.

'A taste,' Anders blurted.

Leah was quiet for a few moments. Anders could hear his son suckling.

'Anders,' Leah finally said, 'I get so much intimacy from feeding Timothy. Sometimes it feels like more than I ever got from sex. By the end of the day, well,' — she looked at Anders — 'I know you need it from me too but it's the last thing on my mind.' Leah sighed. 'Hang on.' When Timothy finished she placed him in his basket on the floor. Anders took off his jeans and settled beside Leah in the bed. He began by kissing her neck, her collarbone, down to her chest, then between her breasts. He licked the left nipple, then the right, which was still warm and damp from his son. He went back to the left and squeezed it lightly. Leah moaned. Timothy whimpered. Leah began to squirm away from Anders.

'God, Leah! Another minute.'

'No, I can't.'

Anders rolled over and let Leah get Timothy. As soon as his son was clamped onto her breast, Anders lost his erection. He stood up and again put on his jeans.

Anders went to the barn to look for his sweater. The fire was still smoking so he poked at the coals and threw on another log. He found both his sweater and the whisky bottle and sat down to drink. Looking at his night fields, at the rows of corn and peas that edged off into the shadows, he could already feel this farm life slipping away from him. Tops, the four acres they farmed might earn them six thousand dollars this year. Add more acres, and that number dropped. Anders figured, at that rate, it wouldn't be long before he'd have to work off the farm to also work on it. Once Timothy was weaned, once the adventure of shopping at Frenchys began to wear thin. Once Leah convinced Anders to have another kid. His sex life had somehow aligned itself with the animals' — rutting and mating seasons, nothing in between.

Anders heard a rustling and went into the barn to check it out. It was dark, black, even after his eyes had somewhat adjusted. He stood very still and closed his eyes and breathed in the smell of hay and old manure. Then he heard the sound again, coming from the loft where Graham and Heidi slept. Rustling. Breathing. A faint moan. He quietly walked to the ladder and climbed the first four rungs. He could hear them both breathing now and began to breathe with them. The breathing stopped. He heard something whispered, a giggle. Then, Graham said, 'You don't have to just listen, Anders.'

Anders's foot slipped and landed on the next rung. He didn't move for over a minute, until he heard them resume. He climbed farther up so he could peek above the floor of the loft. Lit silvery-blue from a solar lantern, Heidi was on her hands and knees with Graham behind her. Heidi's hair covered her face as her head was pushed into the pillows. Graham, wearing his wool work socks and nothing else, leaned over to cup both of her breasts in his hands. When he straightened, he slapped Heidi's ass and turned to Anders and grinned. With his left hand he waved Anders over.

Anders shook his head but slowly climbed the ladder. Once in the loft, he took off his sandals and walked over to and sat on the bunk. Graham continued to fuck Heidi, who reached over to Anders, found his fly and unzipped his jeans. Anders stood up, slid out of his jeans, then sat again on the bunk.

'I can't reach,' he heard Heidi say into the pillow. The bed stopped moving and Anders felt a hand on his balls. He looked down and realized it was Graham's.

'I don't think —'

'Heidi, you take over.'

Heidi got down on the floor and knelt in front of Anders. Anders leaned over and grabbed Heidi's breasts, which were smaller and less full than Leah's. He fought disappointment, tried to pretend Graham wasn't behind him, but his erection began to deflate.

'Shit,' he said.

'Relax,' Heidi said. She worked for a few more minutes, then stopped, sighed, and looked at him.

'Tell me what to do,' she said.

Anders hung his head.

'I'm sorry,' he said. He stood up and found his jeans. By the time he was dressed again, Graham had taken his place on the bunk, Heidi's head between his thighs.

'My turn,' Anders heard Graham say.

Anders watched Heidi's long, silver, naked back disappear as he climbed back down the ladder.

Outside the barn, Anders found his sweater and used it to wipe his forehead. There was a movement, he noticed, by the firepit. The stray dog was back, sniffing around for scraps. Anders picked up a couple of stones and threw them at the dog. The dog hopped sideways, then scampered off into the darkness.

'Git!' Anders yelled after it.

'How many chickens do you have?' Heidi asked Anders at lunch. Anders took a bite from his sandwich and thought.

'Uh, nine egg-layers and eighteen meat birds. Why?'

'I went to get eggs this morning and it didn't seem there were as many. I tried to do a count and only came up with seven hens. Do they go somewhere else?'

'No. Shit. You're sure?'

'Yeah, come on.'

Anders followed Heidi to the chicken coop on the west side of the barn. Her light brown hair, usually tied up in one or two ponytails or braids, hung loosely around her shoulders. He remembered Graham pulling her hair last night, he remembered that hair sweeping his thighs, and then he shook those memories out of his head.

At the coop, seven birds scratched and cooed over the dried grass. Not nine.

'And you locked them up last night? Tightly?'

'No. Isn't that Leah's job? I just did it that one night for her as a favour —'

'Fuck.' Anders kicked at the ground. Two chickens cackled and flapped their red wings in protest. Anders paced and circled the area as Heidi watched.

'Anything I can do?' she asked.

Anders found something and bent down.

'How are you at tracking stray dogs?' he asked, standing up to show Heidi the dismembered foot of one of the chickens.

'I don't want you to kill it!' Leah yelled down the basement stairs. She was jiggling Timothy who had started to cry when Anders slammed into the house.

'We have two fewer hens,' Anders said, coming up the stairs with his rifle. 'Do the math. At this rate we'll have none by Christmas.'

'We'll be fine,' Leah said, eyeing the gun. 'Both Ina next door and Marie on Mill Road get so many eggs, I'm sure we could trade a loaf of bread for a dozen.' Leah's voice started to quaver and Timothy cried louder.

'What, this is the one time he doesn't get your tit?' Anders said.

Leah's eyes widened and her face flushed. Then, very suddenly, she stomped on his left foot. It didn't hurt Anders but it did surprise him. He dropped the gun, which clattered onto the hardwood floor. Leah screamed and nearly dropped Timothy. Anders leaped and caught his arm. For a second, Timothy stopped crying and bobbled his wet, red head between his parents, who each held him under one of his arms. Then Anders handed his son back to Leah. Timothy started to wail and Anders bent to pick up the gun.

'Wasn't loaded,' he muttered as he left the house.

Graham was waiting for Anders by the barn.

'I saw it right here, just last night,' Anders said, sitting down and pulling bullets out of his pocket. 'Ran off in that direction.'

'We're rangers now. Gonna track it through the cornfield.' Graham clapped his hands down on his knees and smiled. Anders continued to load bullets into the gun. Heidi arrived from the garden.

'Seems so vigilante,' she said. She looked at Graham. 'So you *are* going?'

'Hell yeah.'

'I shoulda known. As if you could resist swaggering through the fields with something loaded.'

Anders ran the bolt closed.

'Ready.' He nodded to Graham and they both got up.

'You're not coming?' Graham said to Heidi. She shook her head.

'I'm gonna check on Leah.'

'Good idea,' said Anders. 'Thank you.'

'You're sure it's a dog,' Graham said, jogging to keep up with Anders. 'Not a coyote?'

'It's a dog.'

'What if it's someone's?'

'Then it's their fault,' Anders called over his shoulder.

'I don't know. I'd be pretty pissed to find someone killed my dog.'

Anders stopped.

'Listen, Graham. You have a kid. You try to grow its food and something threatens that — actually destroys what you've built up? You'd want to get rid of that threat.'

'I just don't know. If someone broke into my apartment and stole all my food from my fridge —'

'This is the country. We don't have apartments.'

'So how much are you helping Leah when you've got one of those in the house?' Graham said, nodding towards the gun.

'Did I ask your opinion? Did I?'

'No, I —'

'No. No I didn't. And you can leave before you cause more trouble.'

Graham put his hands in his pockets and stepped away from Anders.

'Never argue with an armed man,' he said, turning back towards the farm. 'Shhhtt, Anders,' Graham suddenly whispered. Anders looked in Graham's direction, and there in the pasture, hidden in the timothy grass, was the stray dog. It did look like a coyote but was blacker, thicker, had floppy ears.

'Anders, I —'

Graham was cut off by the gunshot. There was smoke between them and a heavy silence, as if every bird, the wind, everything around them had stopped. They jogged towards the target.

The first thing Anders heard was the smacking of its mouth, like the sound he made after vomiting. For a moment, Anders felt thirsty and forgot where he was.

'Anders.'

Anders stood above the stray dog. The bullet had gone through its throat and now the dog lay in a growing puddle of its own blackish blood. Its teeth and tongue were frantic and shone with saliva. It was all Anders could look at. The dog fixed its eye on Anders. In the eye wasn't fear, not anger, but, Anders thought, surprise.

'Jesus, you gotta kill it,' Graham said. Anders said nothing. He just watched as the dog lifted its head, then laid it in the blood, its chest and ribs heaving, slower and slower.

'Anders. Anders?' Graham nudged Anders's arm with his elbow. Still Anders didn't move. Finally, Graham grabbed the gun that hung loosely from Anders's hand, put the muzzle flush above the dog's eye, closed his own eyes and pulled the trigger. Anders never looked away.

They buried the dog in the pasture. The sun set. Anders returned home and showered. He found Timothy sleeping in his crib, his little fists clenched, his eyes moving under their thin lids. Dreaming of milk and bread and clucking chickens. Anders leaned into the crib and kissed his soft, warm head.

Leah was sitting up in bed, staring at the door, arms crossed. Anders sat beside her and sighed.

'Did you — ?'

Anders leaned over and pulled Leah's hands away from her chest. He hid his face in her palms and quietly began to cry. Leah pulled him to her chest, and kissed his wet, heavy head.

'It's part of life here,' she said.

Graham and Heidi were gone by the time Anders led the cow into the barn the next morning. They were WWOOFers, Anders reminded himself. They weren't the first to leave without saying goodbye. Anders fastened the cow and listened to her munch hay. Then he began to brush her, first her neck, around her barrel body, under to her belly, down her legs. He didn't hear Leah and Timothy come in.

'They're gone?' she asked. Anders jumped, and the cow briefly paused her chewing.

'They're gone,' he said. 'You're up early.'

'Farm life goes on,' she said. She handed Timothy to his father and sat on the stool. 'I don't think I've milked her in a couple of months. Got enough of my own.' She pressed the cow's teats, spraying milk into the bucket. Anders watched for a few minutes, holding Timothy at his hip. In Timothy's hand was a soggy piece of bread. 'Heidi told me about the other night,' Leah eventually said.

Anders sat on the ground and put Timothy between his legs.

'And?'

'And.' Leah stopped milking and turned to him. 'And it actually made me laugh. Okay, I was mad too, but, well, also sad, you know? Who said babies cement a relationship? They lie. I could lose you but I'm too exhausted to realize it.'

Anders paused.

'I don't know if I should be embarrassed, angry or relieved.'

'Try relieved.'

'I'm sorry,' Anders said. 'I —'

'I'm sorry too,' Leah said, turning back to the milking. 'Ah, kills the hands.' She stopped and stretched them. Anders slid over to Leah and took her hands and began to rub them. 'Your hands don't cramp up?' asked Leah.

'I practise on myself.' He grinned and looked at Leah. 'When will I start feeling like his dad?' Timothy gah-ed and squealed.

'It'll happen,' Leah said. 'In no time he'll follow you around like a shadow, he'll cry when you leave and run to you when you come home. You'll be his hero precisely because you're not me. Just in time too. You're one tiring little guy, Timothy.'

Timothy smiled and wobbled his head. Anders stood him up and kissed his cheeks.

Leah got off the milking stool and sat beside Anders and Timothy. She reached around Timothy and hugged them both. Timothy squirmed between them. When she let go, Anders picked up his son and placed him inside a pen that Anders had recently cleaned and mended. Then he unhitched the cow and led her outside. He returned to Leah who was still sitting on the floor, and began kissing her lips, her ears, her neck. He lifted her sweater and she let him take it off. She unzipped his jeans.

They heard Timothy babble.

'We're right here,' Anders called.

What Zoë Knows

Zoë has always snooped. First at Christmas, looking for presents. Then at her parents' parties, past her bedtime, lying on her belly at the top of the stairs. She went through drawers. Read letters and notes. Listened in on the phone extension.

'Zoë? Is that you?'

She stopped breathing. She tiptoed. She disappeared.

Mostly, what she found was the minutiae of life's minutes, cast-off and forgotten. Conversations flatlined. Then, like an archaeologist in the desert, she found evidence of past civilizations! Black lacy underwear. A dirty birthday card. An old love letter. Tiny empty rum bottles between her mom's sweaters. A wig. And in her dad's truck, condoms. Lubricated. *Ribbed for her pleasure.*

Whose pleasure? Not her mother's. Elise had had her tubes tied twelve years ago.

Zoë shoved them back into Walt's glove compartment and slammed the lid.

Condoms. Zoë found them used in the park, buried in the sandbox. Spent balloons, shrivelled like shed skin. Gross. But gross is what piqued Zoë's curiosity. With only three months until her first day of high school, Zoë wanted to get to the bottom of gross.

Zoë wouldn't have asked if her mom hadn't been into her second glass of wine. And of course there was no way she'd ask Walt.

'Mom, what exactly is a "woman's pleasure"?'

'Christ, Zo, you're barely thirteen.'

'So.'

'So you've got a few years to go before you have to worry about what women worry about.' Elise leaned over to the coffee table and grabbed her wineglass. Zoë had to hurry. By glass number three, her mother wouldn't be so friendly or make as much sense.

'Well, I'm getting a head start,' she said.

'Good.' Elise nodded, then drained her glass. 'Way to take the initiative. Your pleasure is in your hands. So to speak.'

At each recess, just weeks before the grade-eight graduation and, more important, the grad dance, there were still gender divisions, but the lines were moving closer, slow and steady, like armies inching towards the enemy. They'd been discouraged from bringing dates but Zoë's classmates began to sit in pairs on the bus, shared the wares of their lunches, passed notes during math. The girls put on extra makeup at recess, then stood at the edge of the field where the boys played soccer and waited to be selected.

Zoë didn't have time to wait. It was rumoured that her crush, Garret, was about to ask Bethany and Zoë hated Bethany. Or, really, hated her big boobs and the attention they got her.

That night, Zoë snuck out to her father's truck and took his box of condoms.

'You gonna ask Bethany to the dance?' Zoë blurted, after Garret had sleepily shuffled up to their bus stop without a backpack or lunch.

'So what if I do,' Garret said, looking for the bus.

'Courtney says Bethany won't do it till she's sixteen.'

Garret turned and looked Zoë up and down.

'So,' he said, spitting into the gutter.

'So you should ask me.'

'I want to go with someone who has tits.'

'Would you go with someone you could fuck?'

Garret's eyes widened. The bus turned the corner.

'Yeah, right,' he said.

Zoë reached into her pocket and pulled out a condom. Garret stared at her open palm, at the small square package, then quickly reached out and closed her fingers around it. The bus squealed to a stop at the curb.

'Put it away,' he said, his face as red as the blinking lights.

Zoë stood at her bedroom window and watched her father fill the lawnmower's gas tank. Fathers were outside — they were lawns and barbecues and oil changes. Suddenly Zoë saw inside him — whispered words and dirty thoughts. More than a landscaper or chauffeur.

Late afternoon, the phone rang. Her dad answered. Zoë waited two minutes, then picked up the extension.

'— twice this week,' a woman was saying.

Then her dad spoke.

'An hour, tops. You'll be home before supper. I'm already hard.'

'Yes,' the woman breathed as Zoë quietly hung up.

Her name, it turned out, was Audra. Zoë and Walt ran into her at the mall.

'Walt!' By the fountain, water gushed, babies cried, music hummed and people chattered. 'Is this your daughter?' She was loud but everyone was loud. She was also young and short. Not much taller than Zoë. She had cropped, light brown hair and large, round breasts. Zoë liked her hair, which was cuter than her mom's long, greying ponytails, but she did not like this woman's breasts, unlike her father, who, she was disappointed to see, kept glancing at them like the boys in her class glanced at Bethany's or Sophie's or Jennifer's. The woman looked at Walt, who was adjusting his watch, whose cheeks were turning red.

'Yes. Zoë. This is. I mean —'

The woman laughed and Walt laughed too. Then, very quickly, she touched Walt's hand. Walt, just as quickly, pulled it away. Still smiling, she offered the same hand to Zoë.

'I'm Audra,' she said, her hand thrust forward, then drooped like a flag without wind.

'I —'

'Shake her hand, Zo.'

'Right.' Zoë grabbed and shook. The hand was cool and soft and firm. Her three middle fingers each bore a large, silver ring.

'I like your rings,' Zoë said.

'Thank you.' Audra looked at the rings as if surprised they were there. 'You didn't tell me your daughter's so grown-up!'

'She graduates at the end of the month.'

'Not high school?'

'No! Grade eight. How old do you think I am?'

Audra giggled. Giggled! Zoë rocked back and forth on her sneakers.

Walt reached into his pocket for his wallet, grabbed a twenty and handed it to his daughter.

'We'll meet back here at two,' he said.

'I —'

'It was nice meeting you, Zoë,' Audra said.

Zoë nodded. She walked away, then ducked into a store and stood behind a rack of dresses. Her father said something and Audra laughed, mouth wide open, hand fluttering to her neck, rings flashing. They parted and briefly, so briefly, Zoë saw her father's hand brush Audra's bum. Brush, then fall away.

'We have to stop at the liquor store,' Walt said as he and Zoë drove away from the mall.

'Can't Mom buy her own booze?'

'Zo —'

'This morning there were three empty wine bottles in the sink! And I found tiny rum bottles.'

'Your mom works hard.'

'So do you.'

Walt slowed at a stoplight. The light turned green.

'Where did you find those rum bottles?'

'In the house. The kitchen.'

'Zoë …' Walt paused. He turned the volume on the radio up, then down. 'Did you go through my truck?'

'No,' Zoë said quickly. 'Why?'

Walt was quiet.

'Your mom asked me to do her a favour,' he finally said. 'She doesn't talk about it more than that. People talk when they're ready. You can't understand till they want you to understand.' Walt looked quickly at Zoë. 'Capisce?'

'Capisce,' Zoë muttered.

'How was the mall?' Elise asked when they got home.

'We ran into a friend of Dad's.'

'Oh?' Elise looked at Walt as he handed her the brown bag. 'Who's that?'

'Brian,' Walt said.

'Brian?' Elise shook her head. 'I thought you said you were working opposite shifts. Walt?' Zoë started to leave the kitchen. 'Wait, Zoë. Someone called for you. A boy.'

'Boy?' Walt looked up.

'Gareth.'

'Garret,' Zoë corrected.

'Right.'

'Well? What did he say?'

'Maybe I forget.' Her mother often teased Zoë like this: withheld something Zoë wanted, catching Zoë's attention like a cat trapping a bird.

'Just tell me,' Zoë said flatly, reluctantly adding 'please.'

Instead Elise turned to Walt.

'All he said was "Tell her to meet me at noon tomorrow. Tell her she'll need her bike." No please or thank you.'

'Who's this boy?' Walt asked.

'Walt. You know him. You know his dad. Down the road. The black truck?'

'Not the one without the muffler?'

'That's the one.'

Walt shook his head.

'Mom,' Zoë interrupted. 'That's all he said?'

'This better not be a date,' Walt said.

'You're one to talk.'

'Zo —' Walt's voice was sharp. Zoë gulped. Elise looked at her daughter, then at her husband.

'You're gonna let her talk to you like that?' Elise asked.

Walt's forehead furrowed. He looked at Zoë for a long time, then turned, pushed past her and left the kitchen.

'Walt?' Elise looked at Zoë. 'What's going on?' she asked her.

'It's not a date. It's homework,' Zoë said.

In Murphy Woods, where a large sign announced a future subdivision, Zoë followed Garret down one path and up another. They stopped under an oak, got off their bikes and sat down.

'You're staring.' Garret's ears were turning red.

'How's this done?'

Garret's fingers slipped up and under the hem of Zoë's shorts.

'Are you already hard?' Zoë asked.

'What?' Garret's hand fell away. He pulled at the legs of his cut-offs. 'Why'd you say that?'

'Isn't that supposed to happen?'

'Take off your shorts.'

'You too.'

They slid out of their shorts and underwear, then lay down. Zoë looked at Garret's penis, which slouched between his legs like a dried fruit.

'Can I touch it?' she asked.

'If I can touch you,' he said.

Garret pressed his hand between Zoë's legs. Zoë raised her bum off the ground and pushed deeper into Garret's hand. She made a fist around Garret's penis and felt it pulse. As Garret climbed on top of her, Zoë's head lolled to the right.

Through the trees, a movement. Zoë screamed, pushed Garret off, jumped to her feet and grabbed her shorts. Her underwear fell to the ground.

'Aw, Zoë! Fuck! I bit my tongue.' Garret's hand went to his mouth, tears in his eyes.

'Georgia!' a man yelled. Zoë pulled on her underwear and Garret got to his feet, wobbled and fell over, his naked butt in the air. A russet dog bounded through the trees, tail wagging. It snorted and sniffed Garret's ass, then squatted and peed. Zoë laughed.

'Georgia!' The dog ran to her owner, who was now on the path in front of the clearing. 'She's friendly,' he called out, smiling. He stopped when he saw Garret pulling on his shorts. He looked at Zoë, then at Garret, then back at Zoë.

'You okay?' he asked her. Zoë nodded and tried not to laugh. 'You sure?' He watched Garret turn around to do up his fly.

'I'm sure,' Zoë said.

The man stood still. Birds sang, his dog panted, smacked her lips, then started to whine.

'Well, okay. My house is the first one at the end of this path. Red brick. If you're not sure.' He and the dog continued down the path.

'Pervert,' Garret sneered. He got on his bike and, without waiting for Zoë, pedalled away.

* * *

Garret was not at the bus stop the next day. He came to school late and ignored Zoë at morning recess. At lunch, Zoë watched him talk to Bethany under a tree in the north yard. By afternoon recess, Bethany and Garret were holding hands.

The next day Zoë went home at lunch.

Walt's truck was in the driveway.

She had to stop herself from peering through the windows. All these secrets were rattling around in her head like something loose on a car. As she parked her bike in the backyard, Zoë heard Walt's truck start up and drive off. Zoë ran down the driveway and stood in the middle of the street. If her dad had a passenger, she couldn't tell. She remembered that Audra was short.

Upstairs, her parents' bed was made. She pulled back the covers. She looked under the bed. She dug through the bathroom garbage, felt each hardened Kleenex; used floss clung to her fingers. She opened cabinets and turned drawers upside down, removed cushions from the couch.

Out of breath, she sat on her bed. At three she got up and walked to the bus stop.

'Garret!'

Garret looked at Zoë but kept walking.

'What's with you and Bethany?'

'What's it to you?'

'I thought we —'

They were almost at his house. Garret stopped.

'We? No. We never. It was a joke. A bet.' Garret stopped and looked at Zoë's chest. 'Get back to me when you have some tits.'

Her mom was in the kitchen when Zoë returned.

'There's a message you weren't at school and the house has been ransacked.'

'I'm not feeling well.' Zoë stared at the floor.

'Bullshit.' Elise grabbed Zoë's chin and pulled her head up. Her voice softened. 'Zoë?'

'I don't want to go to the grad dance.' Zoë's voice cracked. Elise dropped Zoë's chin.

'That's it? You don't want to go to a stupid dance so you skip school to wreck the house?'

'It's not a stupid dance!'

'Oh, Zoë, don't be ridiculous —'

'It wasn't Brian at the mall on Saturday.'

Elise reached behind her head and took the elastic out of her hair. Her whole face appeared to loosen.

'What are you talking about?' she finally, quietly, asked.

'I found condoms in Dad's truck. I heard him on the phone! I —'

'Zoë, stop.'

Elise went to the fridge and pulled out a half-empty bottle of white wine, then filled a glass. She sat at the kitchen table.

'I already know, Zoë,' she finally said. 'This is a small house, isn't it? I don't want to know what you know.' Elise sipped her wine. 'Listen. Don't talk to him about it. Okay?'

Zoë stared at a stain on the floor. She didn't want to cry. She didn't want her mom to hug her. She just wanted to go to her room and close the door. Elise finished her glass.

'Marriage is not happily ever after. Forget all that shit I read you. Promise you won't hate him. Or me. Promise?'

'Yeah,' Zoë muttered.

'What'd she look like?' Elise asked. 'His *friend*.'

'She —'

'No. Don't tell me. I don't want to know.'

At graduation, Zoë didn't understand all the tears. As she watched Courtney and Bethany cling to each other, their pastel satin dresses rustling, their makeup running, she couldn't wait for high school.

They called Zoë's name and she bounced up the stairs in her sneakers and fancy purple dress. As she received her diploma and shook the principal's hand, she looked into the audience and right at her parents. Both clapped hard, both smiled fiercely, but they looked smaller, flatter — grey and fading. Diploma in hand, Zoë took her seat. She hadn't thought this ceremony would make her feel different. But here she was, the rolled-up paper getting damp in her fist. They called Garret's name. On the stage he raised his arms and her class cheered. She remembered him stumbling, his ass in the air, the dog's nose in his butt. She suddenly laughed. Someone shushed her. Garret scowled into the audience and Zoë grinned.

Diving for Pearls

You ask your dad if he could use an extra hand this season. He asks you if you've had one chopped off since the last time he saw you. While you wait on the phone for his answer, you don't mention that the sight of fish makes you nauseated, that you're doing this just for the EI, that you got stupid in love with a guy in Belize and now, almost three months pregnant, you need time to decide what to do. You hear him crank open the door of his wood stove and toss in a log. You hear your brother, Kevin, in the background, ask, 'Who is it?'

'Kevin could use the company,' your dad says.

The first morning of the autumn lobster season is a race your dad chooses to lose. At most the *Luna Sea* can hold one hundred and twelve traps. Other crews on boats this size make two trips, one now, one twelve hours later on the next high tide.

'Waste of diesel, waste of time,' your dad says, 'and you can't get either back. Plus, good spots will be there tomorrow. Have you ever known a lobster to stick to one place?'

You started fishing with your dad when you were thirteen. After graduation, tired of the rain, the fog, the mould, the moss, the mist, you headed for dry land. You harvested wheat on the Saskatchewan prairie, you mended fences in the Australian outback, you picked grapes in Napa Valley. Your lips chapped, your heels cracked, your fingers callused, your skin bronzed. When your hair was too dry you shaved it off. You shared your bunk, your cot, your sleeping bag with younger boys, older men, one woman. It was Raeka who led you back to water. She had a brother who dove off Ambergris Caye.

'About twenty more,' your dad yells up to you. Your job this morning is to lower traps from the dock, via winch and line, down to your dad and brother in the boat. It is almost seven and the sun has yet to wake up, though the night black is finally fading into the mauve of a cloudy day. Already your wool sweater is soggy, stinks of sweat and the mackerel bait your dad purposely lets rot. You lean over the dock and, just missing the side of the boat, barf into the tide, which swiftly sweeps it away.

'Lightweight!' Kevin heckles.

'You can do this?' your dad asks.

You wipe your mouth on the sleeve of your sweater. You hook another trap into the winch and start the motor.

'Bait's too long in the sun!' you shout.

You've moved into the *Vicki Joan* — your dad's first boat, named after your mother; she still sits in the yard, white and red paint peeling from her wooden hull. Replaced by faster and lighter fibreglass, these old boats were retired to pasture on front lawns and empty lots. After your mother left, you spent time, like you do now, under a heavy layer of blankets inside her weathered cabin. Now you are reading about the expectations of expecting. At the library, it was all you could find. Lots of books for mothers-to-be; none for mothers-who-do-not-want-to-be. Your breath steams up the windows. Your baby, you read, is the size of a strawberry, your uterus, the size of a grapefruit. You could drink twelve strawberry-grapefruit smoothies.

Your brother knocks twice on the port side of the *Vicki Joan* when he arrives for breakfast. You crawl out of the cabin, clamber down the ladder and follow your brother into the house for your dad's high-protein wood stove fry-up: eggs and bacon and sausage. Three months ago you were still a vegetarian, sick of the fish you grew up on. Now all you crave is death.

'Warm enough in there?' Kevin asks through a mouthful of scrambled eggs.

'It's like I'm sleeping under a dentist's X-ray vest,' you answer.

'Or in a coffin,' your dad mutters, swishing maple syrup into his coffee.

You choose, as you have many times before, to ignore him. Instead, you ask, 'How's this season compared to last?'

'Same as the last few years: down.' Your dad shrugs. 'Could be something old, something new, something blue. Warmer waters. Cooler currents. I say it's scallop trawlers clear-cutting the ocean floor, the new fish farm dumping excreta into the harbour, oil, pails, rope, pop cans getting pitched over the sides of boats. D'ya ever see how many tampon applicators are on the beach? How do they get there?' Your dad looks at you accusingly.

'Dad,' Kevin interrupts, 'no lobster ever minded a bit of garbage. Hell, pissing in each other's faces is a turn-on. Jimmy swears he once pulled up a lobster that was chewing on a human hand.'

You stay quiet. If your dad keeps going, it could make for a moody day on the boat. Two flies stupidly buzz and bump into the kitchen window looking for a warm place to hide. Your dad points his fork at Kevin.

'Your friends have no idea that this is how it's going to be. They think fishing will always be there just 'cause it was for their dads and granddads.'

'You think those guys are my friends? Dad thinks Jimmy and his brothers are now my friends 'cause I scalloped with them for three days in August.' Kevin turns to your dad. 'And I could be earning a hell of a lot more money if you shut up about scalloping when they were around.' Kevin puts his fork down with a clatter. 'Last day I was out with them, we were getting into the harbour and just past the bell buoy they told me to get out and swim.'

'You coulda said no,' you say.

'You know those guys. They basically pushed me in.'

You do know those guys. It's what Kevin doesn't know. Another reason you left, to get away from Jimmy and his brothers.

A high school party close to graduation on the beach at Kettle Cove. Everyone was drunk. You wandered off with Jeremy. You liked Jeremy. He was funny, cute, made you laugh in class. Unlike his brother Shane, who was also in your class because he'd failed a grade, who said he couldn't wait to fish with Jimmy full-time.

'Took me almost an hour to swim back,' Kevin is saying, 'and fuck I was cold when I got to the dock, even in the survival suit. Climbed up the ladder and quit.'

You were far from the fire so the beach was dark. You started it. You kissed Jeremy. And he kissed back. Hard. He unzipped your jeans and you reached for his.

Too soon he was done. Just as you were getting started. He left you to make your own way back to the fire. When you got there, Jeremy was standing beside Shane and wouldn't look at you. But Shane did. He looked and grinned. You grabbed your jacket and started to leave.

'I thought I was next!' Shane called after you, and everyone around the fire, including Jeremy, laughed.

You considered revenge. Instead, you graduated and left the village. You were done with water, with beaches, with boats and the stories that spread on them, hauled into shore like the catch from traps. Done, until you met Diego.

'What you do, Dad,' Kevin says, 'has consequences, just like what they do. Now if I wanna scallop —'

'How did I raise you two to be fishermen?' your dad interrupts. 'How did that happen?'

Kevin snorts as he pushes his chair from the table. Your dad grabs his wrist but turns to you.

'Promise me you'll never, ever let your kids fish. Promise!'

'Yeah, I promise,' you say quietly.

'Better yet, don't have any kids. I swear if you do, and they're fishing, I'll come back and fucking haunt you.' He gets up from the table and takes your unfinished plate.

Two knocks on the port side of the *Vicki Joan*. You manage to bury your baby-name book just as your dad squeezes and ducks into the cabin.

'Don't let in any flies,' you say.

'There's plenty of room in the house,' he offers.

'I like it here.'

'I can see my breath.'

'People live in igloos.'

'Not since we called them Eskimos.' He holds up a space heater and extension cord. 'This won't help much in January.'

'Season ends by Christmas.'

'And then what?'

You shrug. 'Get on a shrimp boat in Florida?'

'EI could help you pay for school. I'd help out a bit.'

'There are other ways to learn. You dropped out.'

''Cause I met your mom.'

''Cause you got her pregnant.'

'You know I loved her.'

'I heard Mom,' you say. 'She chose this life, she chose to have me, and she said, over and over, it was the death of her.'

'It's awful she said that to you.'

You shrug.

'You were on the boat,' you say. 'All the time. So I heard what she had to say.'

'So now she's gone you're tagging into her fight? Think about it' — your dad's voice gets louder — 'and stop thinking about her for one second. Yes. She complained all the time about having you two. Like it was only hard on her. But it was hard on both of us. We both had to give up so much. The difference is I thought you were worth it. She didn't. So she left.' His fist flies out and hits the side of the *Vicki Joan*. You jump. He pauses, looking at your shape under the blankets. 'What about you?' he asks quietly. 'There are a thousand other things you could do than be here. Why'd you come back?'

'For time, Dad,' you say, sighing. 'For time to consider the options. Right now, fishing is easy.'

'Stop pretending. This life is not easier and you know it. Your mom let you know it.' He opens the cabin door and a fly darts in. 'That's what I don't get. That you're actually considering having this baby. If that's what you decide, then let me tell you now: keep this baby and you can no longer fish on my boat.'

Diego guessed you were pregnant before you could tell him.

'You haven't bled in two months.'

'I kept hoping I would.'

He knew your body better than you — your blemishes, bruises, birthmarks and periods. No blood in the water. He counted the moles on your back. He noticed how quickly your hair grew. He knew which breast was slightly larger, and how tickling its nipple made you come. This scrutiny, like that of the tides, of the sun, of the seasons, was an extension of his job. You spent more time together naked than clothed.

And then, sure you were pregnant and sure he would know, you tried to hide. In baggy T-shirts and his cut-off jeans, as if you were already showing.

'I love you. I will love this baby,' he said.

'I'd have to stop diving. We'd have to change.'

'I would,' he said.

You left. Before he could change. Before the pregnancy changed you.

Sick of change, you got on a bus and headed back to the place you thought never changed.

Four hours into your day on the water, a southeasterly gale picks up, which strengthens the tide and drowns your dad's orange-and-yellow buoys. The wind brings sideways rain, then hail, then sun, then snow. You've called it a day and are now anchored in Kettle Cove to wait for high tide.

You never get seasick. Never. You blame your queasiness on morning sickness. Sitting near the stern on an upturned bait box, you picture your little strawberry, bobbing in its own warm fluid, curled like a shrimp, your darkness, your heartbeat, your muffled voice its whole world. *Better this world inside you?* you wonder, staring at Kettle Cove beach, recalling that night with Jeremy and Shane, your nausea increasing. You could make it so this not-quite-world was the baby's only world, so its time on the planet wasn't ever on it but only in you. As the waves around you chop and hiss over the side of the *Luna Sea*, you grow jealous, not of the baby's warm, liquid world but of its ability to breathe within it.

As if you evoked them, around the corner of the cove creep Jimmy's brothers on their boat. Your father has anchored too close to their traps.

'Great,' says Kevin. He stops filling bait bags and disappears into the wheelhouse. You straighten your toque but stay seated as the boat pulls alongside yours. You've been expecting to meet them and you will not hide. Besides, nowhere to hide on the water except under the surface.

'Afternoon,' says Jimmy. You wave a gloved hand. 'How's she goin'?'

'Bobbing along.' You smirk.

'Your dad aboard?'

'Of course.' You stand up.

'Could I have a word?'

'Could have it with me.'

'Don't have much to say to you.'

'Is that your opinion or your brother's?' you ask.

'Didn't you leave?' Jimmy asks as Shane joins him on the deck. He looks at his brother and grins. 'Or did you come back for more?'

Your nausea is replaced by rage. You want to jump onto their boat and strangle them both. All three. You can see Jeremy in the wheelhouse, watching you as he revs the throttle to keep the boat in place.

Your dad appears at your side. You move towards their boat. Your dad's arm gently rests on your shoulder. You back up, moving towards the bait barrels.

'What can I do you for, Jimmy?' your dad asks.

'Having troubles?' Jimmy asks.

'Just waiting on the tide.'

'Then how's about waiting somewheres else. Got some traps to check. Unless you poached 'em already.'

'Now, Jimmy, I was about to move till you said that. If there's anything in them, it's not going anywhere.'

'You mind telling me how all my empty oil pails ended up back in my boat the other day?'

'That's the funny thing about dumping shit into the ocean. You think it's big enough, it'll just go away, and then there it is. Odd winds lately.' Your dad looks at the sky, its mix of grey and white clouds. Jeremy revs their boat's engine again. It is only three metres away.

'You're all fucking crazy,' Shane yells.

You ignore him. You are removing the lid of the barrel in front of you. The rot hits your nose and gut like a punch.

'Move your boat,' Jimmy says.

'I was thinking of it. But that "crazy" crack.' Your dad shakes his head.

'Fuck.' Jimmy spins his finger in the air and Jeremy launches the boat forward and around to your starboard side. Her wake lurches the *Luna Sea* sharply sideways and back. You tumble onto your ass but quickly get up. Suddenly Kevin is by your side. You toss him a bait bag and nod. Laughing, cackling, like the kids you once were, you throw the putrid bags at Jimmy and Shane. One splats in the middle of Shane's back.

'Ass fucks!' Kevin hollers.

'Stop it, both of you,' your dad warns. You grab another mesh bag from the barrel but your stomach has had enough. The smell of it makes you gag. You move to the portside in case you puke.

'She's pregnant. Pregnant!' Kevin, red-faced, stomping, is yelling at Jimmy and Shane and pointing at you.

'Kevin,' you snap, glaring at your dad.

'Can't keep your legs together?' Shane yells.

Before you can respond, Kevin clambers into the wheelhouse and starts the engine.

'Kev, the anchor!'

He does not hear. He is pushing the *Luna Sea* into full throttle towards the brothers' boat. When he rams the nose into her side, the weight of the anchor snaps her back, almost dragging her under water. You stumble and fall over the side and into the frigid bay.

Diego taught tourists to dive but because you were a friend of his sister, for you he waived his fee. When you first fell back from his boat and into the water, first opened your eyes, you couldn't believe you were under water. Compared to the murky, tide-churned Bay of Fundy, inhabited by anti-social lobsters, the Caribbean Sea is more clear and blue than a cloudless sky, more colourful and teeming than spring. You had one word for Diego when you resurfaced.

'Fiesta,' you said.

He taught you that the barrier reef is alive, is a fed-on and feeding animal, is a giant skeleton of skeletons. You dove deeper and longer, joined groups of groupers, encouraged a parrotfish onto your shoulder. You grew frustrated by the limits of your lungs. You never wanted to surface. Raeka left for California. You did not join her.

Your brother graduated from high school. He emailed to say he'd joined your father on the boat. He asked you when you were coming home. You touched the keyboard and felt the cold Fundy wind in your fingers. You sent a one-word response: *never.*

You slept each night on the beach with Diego.

'Every part of me feels alive,' you said.

Two weeks later you were pregnant.

The chattering of your teeth wakes you up. Where are you? In a bed. Yellow walls, fluorescent lights.

'I'm cold,' you say.

'Thank God.'

'Didn't Dad raise us to be atheists, Kev?'

'The nurse wants to know how far along you are. How many weeks? She asked if you'd seen a doctor. She said Dr Bittorf would be here on Monday, nine till three.'

'When did Dad tell you?'

'A couple days after the season started. Said I should try to do more of the work without letting on that I knew.'

'And screaming it at Jimmy and Shane is "not letting on"? Who told Dad?'

'Diego called.'

You notice Kevin's hair is wet.

'You jumped in.'

'Ball shocker.' He grins, then stops and leans closer to your face. 'Listen, Dad sold his licence two weeks ago. Just before you got home. Some guy from Big Cove reserve. It's done. We're done. Last season.'

'Shit,' you say. 'One less option.'

You move into the house and onto a couch beside the wood stove. It takes you two days to warm up. You tell your dad you're ready to go out again.

'I can get another guy,' he says, sitting beside you.

'This gal will do the work of two guys. You shoulda said you sold your licence.'

'You shoulda said you were pregnant. I have to find out from your boyfriend. He wants to marry you?'

'What am I gonna do, raise a baby in a hut on the beach? Get Diego to come here? He's from Mexico. He won't survive a frost, let alone winter.'

'Wynne and Ivan lived in a yurt with their kids.'

'That was the sixties.'

'It was the late seventies.'

'You gonna kick me out?'

'No, but staying here is the easy way out, and —'

'Why fish when I could dive for pearls.' You search through your pockets for a card the nurse gave you. 'Could you pass me the phone?'

Your dad drives you to Truro because you won't be able to drive home. You are both quiet. You follow the coast, which follows the highway. You realize it's been six years since you've been on this steep and winding road; you feel each drop and curve in your already uneasy belly. You look out the window and there is road, then shoulder, then guardrail, then nothing but whitecaps, the sea thrashing miles below.

You crest Economy Mountain, the last peak before the road descends out of the pass to run parallel to the shoreline. To your left the Cobequid Hills roll orange and green and fade and blur into farm and forest. At right, the Minas Basin at low tide lies long and flat and red and muddy, contrasted with broken black cliffs and the egg, diamond and pinnacle islands some say were tossed in place by an angry, giant Aboriginal god.

'Diving in the Caribbean, I thought, *This is life*. I couldn't imagine coming back here. It just felt so, well, dead. But Dad' — you gesture towards the Bay of Fundy, its blue-grey water once again following the moon back to shore — 'when I fell overboard and went under, all I could think was: *survive*. There *is* life here, and I wanted to fight for it.'

'You sure you want to do this,' he says.

'No, I'm not sure. I'll never be sure.'

'I can turn around. Just tell me.'

You put your hands in your lap.

'When I got pregnant, I thought my only options were kill or be killed. You're right. Mom shouldn't have said what she said to me. Have the baby or not — either decision, I'm realizing, can open up my life. I was stupid, I wasn't careful, but that doesn't mean I have to stop living, does it? Am I being selfish?'

'Not at all.'

'I want to go find Diego, eventually. If I can. And if not, well ...'

The sun pops above the horizon, small and distant now but still sharply red. Your dad lowers his sun visor and sits taller in his seat.

'If not, what?'

You close your eyes against the glare.

'Well, wherever I end up, it'll be by the water. I can't imagine living anywhere else.'

An Unkindness of Ravens

Mark was at the desk in the spare room, busy with his children's book, hunched over the paper and watercolours. I put my hand on his shoulder blade.

'I like the crow.'

'It's a raven.' He shrugged my hand away.

'Okay, raven. So why ravens?'

Mark sighed. He'd been doing that a lot lately. He didn't look up from the paper.

'I've always liked them. And then I started reading more about them, how smart they are, how they can form these tight family units. I don't know, Justine. The story just came after that.'

Mark and I'd been living together about four months. It was my longest relationship, Mark's second-longest. As soon as he moved in, I couldn't help talking marriage and family. I'd turn it into a joke but we both knew I wasn't joking.

'Family?' I tried not to sound too hopeful.

'Raven family,' Mark said flatly.

I glanced again at the desk and fingered a binder. 'What's this?'

'Research for the book.'

'Can I look at it?'

'If you want.'

I flipped through the pages of photocopies, sketches and scribblings. *Common raven or corvus corax ... adult, three feet, beak to tail ... trickster, creator ... shapeshifter ... bearer of bad news ...*

'You using the truck today?' he asked.

I closed the binder and stood beside Mark again, my hand light on his shoulder.

'It needs gas. Why?'

'I want to go to South River.'

'Because?'

'There's a woman there looks after hurt ravens.'

'That sounds cool.'

'Well, I'll just be taking pictures. It won't be too exciting.'

My palm circled the back of his pilling green sweater, over his sharp shoulder blades. Wings ready to burst.

'So ... can I take the truck?' Mark asked.

'Until these wings are ready to sprout, yes. But I'm coming too.'

I had moved to North Bay to finish my bachelor's. Mark, after many weekend visits, had eventually followed, so we knew Highway 11 by instinct. My truck was old but a new acquisition, a parental donation to help with our move once my year was finished. Forty minutes to South River, the length of my thumb on a road map. At the side of the highway, the trees were beginning to green and bud. I left the heater off.

Highway 11. A grey, cracked, asphalt line blasted out of the pink shield rock. I had once waited an hour in summer-construction traffic as they set off dynamite to expand the highway into four lanes. Bumper-to-bumper trailers, minivans, hitched boats. People getting out to walk dogs, pee, throw Frisbees. Suddenly *poomf,* then heads turning to the louder *brrashttt* of raining stones that sent birds squawking into the air and the people and dogs into their cars. Fifteen more minutes and we'd inched ahead, my arm dangling out the window, towards the new landslide of rocks.

'When I was a kid, my parents and I were stuck here for over an hour in traffic. I remember people —'

'You've told me,' Mark said.

'Oh. Oh, yeah.' I was driving, Mark was stiff in the passenger seat, hands cupped and squeezed between his thighs. I pointed to the right.

'New moose-crossing sign.'

'Oh yeah?'

'Night danger,' I read.

'What?'

'Moose.' While my profs had told horror stories of animal-car collisions, what I'd always found more frightening was the blackness that sucked in light like gravity. One night, outside Powassan, Mark and I had traded driver for passenger and I couldn't get into the truck fast enough, running around the hood, chilled by the shivering sound of crickets.

I sped us beside blurred white pines, balsam firs, hemlock and spruce — brown-tipped from sprays of winter salt. Bleached birch shafts. It was one thing to leisurely collect spring sap from the spaced maples of southern woodlots, another to wander into these dense coniferous forests, lose direction and panic.

'If you were dropped into the middle of that bush, do you think you'd be able to make it out?'

Mark turned to the dizzy trees.

'What are you asking?'

A month into our relationship, before I even knew the name of Mark's first pet (or whether he had had one at all), we quit our jobs to backpack across Canada.

'This is spontaneous,' I said on the stern deck of the *Chi-Cheemaun*, 'but wouldn't it be crazier to come back married by the ferry captain?'

'I don't think captains can marry people anymore,' he mumbled slowly. The boat lurched and Mark lost balance, paled, then puked into the wake over the railing.

'Oh, Mark, are you okay?' I tried not to smile.

'I can't believe this is worse than the ferry to Vancouver Island.' Mark heaved and I rubbed my hand down his spine. Gulls followed, eager for more.

'Why would it be?'

'It crosses an ocean.'

'You don't know the Great Lakes.'

On land, Mark managed better. He came bouncing out of the check-in cabin at Lake Superior Park as I was fanning outhouse smell from my nose.

'Good news. The Parks girl says there are two sites left. One's a kinda bowl, the other's on a hill. I chose the bowl. It sounded more comfortable.'

'What if it rains?' I gazed at the towering curls of cumulus.

'The girl said there's only a forty percent chance. She was really funny. Said she'd puked on the ferry as well.' We tugged on our backpacks and started walking.

'Is she cute?'

'Huh?'

'Your ranger girl. Would you fuck her if I wasn't here?'

Mark stopped unfolding the park map.

'What are you talking about? You're crazy.'

'You love that I am.'

'I'm beginning to realize.'

It was August and even the northern nights were humid. In just our underwear, Mark and I lay on top of the gluey sleeping bags, the tent fly open, listening to raccoons snuff around our site, crickets chirp and echo.

'Do you really want to get married?' Mark asked.

'Now?'

'No, not now.'

'To you? Mark, are you proposing?'

'No. No.' His body shifted until his face was over mine. The DEET smell was biting. I could dimly see the outline of his hat-matted hair. 'Someday I mean. You think about it.'

'I do and I don't. I *would* like to spend a lot of time with you.'

'So if I proposed right now you'd say yes.'

'You *are* proposing.'

Mark sighed.

'Oh I don't know,' I continued. 'If I said no and you went away because of that, I'd reconsider it, sure.'

'Even though we've been together a month?'

'You're special. Dog, house, family. Seems you'd be a natural part of that.' I reached under the elastic of his boxers to tease his damp balls. 'Why are you asking?' I whispered.

'Mmm, never mind.' His lips opened around my ear.

'Hey, is that rain?' I sat up.

'Hmm?'

'Listen.' Drops tapped the tent's roof, their slow walk moving quickly to a march. 'Shit. You put the ground sheet under the tent?'

'I thought it'd make the tent hotter.'

'Are you serious? We're in a *bowl*. Bowls collect water.'

'Oh, come on, we'll be fine. The rain sounds great.'

'It won't feel great.'

By morning, after a night of near-floating, one of the only things not wet was the ground sheet in which we wrapped the dripping tent, packed up, and caught a taxi to a motel in Wawa. The next day we were on a bus home.

* * *

My rusty truck rattled on as I slid *Abbey Road* into the tape deck, trying to drown out the sound of the missing muffler by singing loudly to 'Because'. For radio stations, we had few choices — CKAT country, EZ Rock, the Wolf. The only reasonable radio station was the CBC but we couldn't sing along to discussions about salamanders, shad flies and Lake Nipissing's low water levels. Today, Mark wasn't singing.

'The turnoff's coming up, first one after the high school,' he said. 'This road.' Mark pointed. 'Here — here's the road.'

'Yeah, yeah. How far?'

We hit gravel. Over train tracks. Trees, trees, one or two bungalows chopped into the landscape. Then brush grass, like the Arctic in summer. Exposed pink-grey rock. Dead grass fields still squashed from the drawn-out weight of snow.

'She raises huskies, too.'

'Hmm?'

'This raven woman. In winter she takes people out dogsledding.'

'Yeah? We coulda gone this winter. Too bad. Mark?'

'This must be the dog farm she said she lives near.'

'Wait. *She* takes people out? *She* lives near? So she lives alone?'

'I didn't ask.'

Passing the first dog farm we could see about fifty dogs anchored individually to bricks by short ropes. Plastic barrels on sides acted as shelters. Some of the dogs — not pure huskies but mutts — stood up, wagged, and barked at us and their neighbours. Others lay still, dozing in dirt patches near mounds of shit, or stood silent and quivering, their tails curled and clinging to their bellies. I slowed the truck at the turn.

'You think they've been out like that all winter?' I asked, thumping through a pothole.

'They're bred for winter.'

'Don't they look, well, distressed? Lonely?'

'They're beside other dogs.'

'It just seems, you know, they'd be happier in a group, sniffing each other's butts —'

'That's stupid.'

'Don't dogs prefer packs?'

'Not the lone wolf.'

I chewed the corners of my mouth. 'I read in your binder that young ravens are social too. They actually pair off around the age of three, flirting by flying in sync.'

'You're doing it again, Justine.'

'What?'

'Your little hints about family. About our future.'

'Just *the* future. You used to, too.'

'Did I? What did I say?'

'You talked about us. About a house. About getting a dog.'

'Was that talking about us or just talking?'

'I don't remember,' I said.

'Me neither.'

'Hey.' I turned to Mark's stiff, granite jaw. 'How did you meet ... what's her name?'

'Lillah. I'm not fucking her. She's in my pottery class.'

'I didn't say you were.'

'You were thinking it.'

'Suddenly you can read my mind?' I sighed. So did Mark. 'Well, did you at least call this raven lady?' I asked.

'No,' Mark said.

'No? So we're just dropping in?'

'I guess.' As we pulled into the driveway, dozens of huskies erupted from long wire pens, leaping, yapping and growling. The older dogs bared their teeth while the puppies clambered through their legs and on top of one another. We got out of the truck.

'Do you think she's here?'

'What?'

The screen door to the house opened and the raven lady appeared. As she clomped in boots down the plank stairs the dogs started to settle, focusing their blue, brown, mismatched eyes in her direction. And so did we.

She was not the raven-haired witch of the woods I'd expected. Her stained jeans, tight and faded, revealed she was more earthy than ethereal. She wore a thick, grey turtleneck, though she didn't have much neck to turtle. She had to be about forty, and for a moment I relaxed, certain Mark had never said he found older women attractive.

'Hey Mark,' she said, her face serious. 'This is a surprise.'

'You said drop in anytime. So, I'm dropping.'

'Did I say that?' Lillah shrugged. 'Country pleasantries.' She looked me up and down. 'Too late in the season for a sled ride.' She scratched the cropped hairline at the back of her neck. Her hair was short and shapeless, blunt-edged as though she'd cut it with wing clippers. Her face, though, was young, ruddy and slightly lined, like a February apple.

Except for the sound of fussing dogs, it was quiet. I waited for Mark to introduce me.

'I ... we came to see your ravens. I brought my camera.' He held it up. 'To, uh, take pictures. Should I have called?'

'Nah. Don't always hear the phone.'

'Oh. Well, sorry to bother you. This is Justine.'

I extended my hand.

'Yep.' Her handshake was quick but strong. She backed away, her deep-set eyes squinting, almost sinking into her face. 'Hey. Hey! Settle down over there.' I jumped, thinking she was talking to me, until the dogs calmed. 'I've only got the one raven right now. He's not more than a year old.'

'I see.' I watched Mark nod. His eyes flicked between Lillah's large, bra-free breasts and her crossed arms. He turned to me and quickly raised and lowered his eyebrows, trying to laugh off the fact I'd caught him looking.

'Well, one's better than none,' I said. I smiled. Lillah didn't.

'Sooo,' Mark tried, 'the raven, he's —'

'The ravens are usually out now.' Lillah stared at the sky across the road. Blank, pale, yellow and blue. Clouds and sky blended. We all stared and my vision shimmered, unfocused.

'Pardon me?'

'They come out around lunch,' she said, not turning her head. 'There's a family that lives in the area — six of them. Around now they come out to play. Chase each other, fight over things they find. They've been coming less and less — but I thought they'd come today.' She turned slightly, and I watched her round head in profile. 'Maybe not 'cause you're here.'

'They wouldn't care,' I spoke. She looked at me.

'Ravens are pretty smart.'

'Oh yeah.' Mark jumped in. 'I've been doing a lot of reading. They can figure out how to open a cooler to get at the food.'

'Can't they learn to speak?' I asked.

'Yeah, and they can imitate the sounds of other animals, and even babies,' Mark said.

Lillah turned to Mark. 'Why do you want to take pictures?'

'I'm working on a kids' book. It's about a raven. I wanna get some good close-up shots for reference.'

'I don't know if that's a good idea.' She looked at his point-and-shoot camera.

'Oh?'

'Well, it's dark down there and the flash would scare him — he's pretty jumpy already.'

Great, I thought, twenty bucks on gas.

'I also brought my sketchbook,' he said.

'Better. Okay, come on.'

Lillah and Mark walked up to the house, entered through the screen door and disappeared. I stood for a second, then moved to follow, but as I looked up, the inside door shut tight. I stayed at the bottom of the steps and put my chilled hands in my jacket pockets.

This jealousy, this possessiveness, this suspicion. I was sick of feeling it constantly. To prove I could get beyond it I stayed where I was, picked up stones and threw them at the truck tires. Some of the stones bounced up against the rust, dropping chips onto the gravel driveway.

I'd been trying to convince Mark that these feelings weren't random — hadn't come out of nowhere. They'd started in December when I went down to Toronto to Mark's parents' for Christmas. In his room, too awake to sleep, listening to his father's nearby snoring (Mark was assigned to the basement couch), I flipped through his art books. From the middle of a new Maurice Sendak biography, a letter fell to the floor. On the envelope, girlish looping writing. I listened for sounds outside the door. Mark's dad wheezed, gasped, snorted. I opened the letter. It was dated December sixth.

I read it twice, my cheeks flaming. Mark came in during the second reading.

'Look what I found,' I said.

'You were snooping.'

'I was reading.'

We argued in whispered tones for almost half an hour.

'You can't stay friends with an ex,' I stated.

'Why?'

''Cause someone's always doing it to get more.'

'That's not true.'

'Then what's this?' I pointed out *I'll always love you, XOXO, Dana* at the bottom of the page.

'Well, that's not always true. And didn't you stay friends with that computer guy?'

'Not for long, maybe a couple of years.'

'So?'

'It's 'cause we never fucked.'

He rolled his eyes. 'Oh come on, how long did you date?'

'A few months.'

'And you never fucked?'

'That's not the point. How do you love someone, then break up and shut that off?'

'You just do. *You* have.'

'Yeah, but sometimes it's still there.' I flicked the letter, pinched in my fingers.

'Okay, so *she* still thinks it's there,' he said.

'Right. And, yeah, I was friends with that guy for a while. Until I met you.' I sighed. 'Is it this long-distance thing?'

'No, but it sounds like you're jealous.'

'No,' I lied. 'Jealous of what? That you're fucking me now instead of her? Or that I never get to see you and I don't know what the hell's going on in your life anymore and what you think or feel?'

He shrugged and shook his head. 'I *love* you. You know that.'

'I *miss* you. I hate this being apart. I hate that you're just a sweaty plastic phone in my hand every night. Now I'm gonna try and call and you'll be out and I'll think "What or who the fuck's he doing?"'

'Then forget it. I hate it here. I'll come back with you to North Bay.'

I swallowed. He kissed me. I cupped my hand to his thin neck. We moved to the floor because the bed would squeak. The overhead light, which appeared and hid behind Mark's shoulder, was too bright so late.

'What'll you do in North Bay?' I asked afterwards as we stretched our carpet-burned backs and knees.

'I don't know. Take art courses at the college. Get another student loan.'

'Maybe you could find a job?' I spread open my palm on his sunken stomach, sliding it through his hairs and our cooling sweat.

'Maybe.'

Now I walked to the husky pens. I tried to convince myself that Lillah was not Mark's type: a bit too old and slightly lumpy, like a duffle bag I'd haul to the laundromat, straps bruising my shoulders. Many of the dogs were asleep now but the puppies were lively. I crouched to them. They came sniffing to the fence. All the dogs were separated into groups — one adult with a litter. A shepherd with a flock, a teacher and tribe, a parent with babies. In the closest pen, the elder's watching eyes were the colour of sky. The pups licked my fingers.

Eventually, suspicion got the better of me. I stood up and, turning, wiped my hands on my jacket, then went up the steps and into the house.

I followed their voices through piles of clutter — brochures, papers, receipts, dirty coffee mugs, opened and unopened bags of dog food that overflowed from every surface and corner — towards the basement stairs. I descended quietly.

'— going on fifteen years,' Lillah was saying. 'Eric's family's from the area. We met at U Guelph.' Lillah turned towards me as I reached the basement. Mark glanced quickly at me, then went back to sketching.

'Eric's your husband?' I asked. Lillah snorted.

'Jeez, no. Never married. Never saw the point. Keeps us free to come and go, you know?'

I saw Mark nod. My heart thudded. Then a black-on-black movement in the corner startled me. The raven.

As my eyes adjusted to the dimly lit basement, I could see the raven standing on a post in a caged-off corner. I stared at its profile, its large hooked beak, its one eye the only part of it that reflected light. I stepped towards the cage to get a better look.

'Don't get too close,' Lillah said. 'He's used to me and Eric, but that's about it for humans.'

'Where'd you find him?' I asked.

'In the woods about a month back. Broken wing's nearly healed. Good thing we got him before the coyotes.'

'And then?'

'Then he'll fly the coop. Back to the unkindness.'

'The what?' I asked.

'Collective noun,' Mark said quickly. 'Like school of fish? Unkindness of ravens.'

'I always loved that,' Lillah said. 'The group, the family, being unkind. Seems about right.'

'You ever get sad when they go?' I asked.

'You'd have to be pretty heartless not to. Must be why I never wanted kids. Empty nest is hard enough when it's just a bird.' She turned to the cage. 'Not that a raven is just a bird.'

'Okay,' Mark said, closing his sketchbook. 'I think I got some good stuff here.'

We left the basement and headed outside to the truck, where Mark turned to Lillah.

'Thank you,' he said, extending his hand. Lillah took it and shook, lingering.

'I'd like a copy of that book when it comes out. Signed,' Lillah said, then suddenly gave Mark a hug.

'Hey Mark,' I interrupted, 'can we get going?'

'Yeah, yeah.' He slouched towards me.

'Your lady awaits.' Lillah laughed and turned towards her house.

'I want to drive,' Mark said once Lillah was back inside.

'Too bad.' I got in the driver's side, put in the key. The truck hacked and burped, starting, and I backed up to the gravel road, just as Mark closed his door on the racket of huskies.

I finally turned to Mark as we stopped at a red light in Powassan. He sat as far away as he could, his body pushed against the passenger door, head turned away. He fingered the cord on his camera. In his lap was a brochure.

'What's that?'

'Hmm?' Not turning.

'The paper.'

'Oh' — sighing — 'it's just some info on dogsledding. List of prices, that kinda thing.' The light turned. I sped ahead.

'So, you hot for Lillah?'

'What?' Now he looked at me. 'What's that supposed to mean?'

'Come on, off you go, alone in the house, I'm not invited. Then that hug.'

'You weren't not invited. And it was just a hug.'

'I think you were making the moves on her. Or she on you.'

'What the hell's your problem?'

'What the hell do you mean? You're the quiet one. I drive you down in *my* truck, no thank you and *I've* got a problem? Fuck you.'

'Fuck you.' He crossed his arms and turned away. I clenched my teeth, blinking fast. Put on my sunglasses. My hands began to sweat on the smooth plastic steering wheel.

Passing Callander, I noticed the fuel gauge, which must have been riding red since leaving South River.

'Didn't you get gas?' I asked.

'Huh?'

'Gas. I gave you twenty bucks? You took the truck out before we left? The truck needed gas.'

'Film was on sale.'

'Okay. Film. And then —?'

'And I came back home. Guess I forgot.'

'You forgot.'

'Mmm-hmm.'

'You're an adult, right? So are you retarded or just stupid? Cars need gas to go. Do *you* know where the fuck the next gas station is?'

Mark crumpled the brochure, strangling it in his fist, then pitched it at my face. I jerked my head to avoid it, swerving the truck into the middle of the two lanes. The paper bounced off my cheek and landed in my lap. I straightened the truck in time to avoid an oncoming transport, then, still sweating, flicked the paper onto the floor where it began soaking in a small puddle. My heart and lungs strained.

Remembering the old highway, now bypassed by the new 11, I turned off ten minutes south of the city. Strip bars, deserted motels, truck stops, gas stations. I chugged into the first one.

'How much you got left of that twenty, Mark?'

He searched his jeans pocket. 'Here's five.'

'Just five dollars of regular,' I said to the attendant, a boy in an oil-smeared red golf shirt, who nodded and did his job.

Returning to the old road, I put my hand on Mark's left thigh.

'Mark? Hey Mark.' I shook his leg.

'Mmnnh.'

'Mark, I'm sorry.' Pause. 'Are you sorry?' Long pause. 'Mark?'

'For what?'

'Oh come on. You've been all fucked-up quiet for almost two weeks. What's going on?' I moved my hand to his shoulder, began to poke. 'Hey pointy-blades? Hey sweet wings, you still love me, right?'

'Look.' He pushed my hand with the back of his. 'I got a call last week for a job at a gallery in Toronto. Training would start in two weeks.'

My stomach turned. 'And?'

'And … I don't know. It's a good opportunity.'

'Yeah, it is. For you. So are you gonna go?' I took off my sunglasses, pushing the truck well beyond the speed limit. 'When the hell were you going to tell me?'

He shrugged. 'It's the gallery where Dana works.'

I paused.

'Your ex? Your ex, *Dana*? What's that fucking mean, Mark?'

Mark was quiet a long time.

'It's a good opportunity,' he finally repeated.

'*It's a good opportunity,*' I tried to mimic. I frowned at my shaking voice. 'And us? What about that "opportunity"? You know I love you.' I reached for the hand rooted in his lap.

'No you don't,' he said.

My hand hung above his.

'Pardon?'

'Look.' Mark stared at the salty windshield. 'We've had fun, we've shared intense feelings, but I guess I can't say I know what love is.'

'Did Lillah say something to you?'

'What? Of course not. But she's got the right attitude, you know? Refreshing. Who the fuck cares about marriage? Why's it gotta be this big deal? Why can't we just live now and not worry about then or later?'

'She did say something to you.'

'I'm so sick of you constantly being suspicious.'

'Seems I've had reason to be.'

'You really think we love each other? Really? All I keep thinking of is the raven book and this new job —'

'More than me.'

'The book is important, Justine. I don't have time for it *and* for you.'

'You don't want to make time,' I choked.

'No. Not here.' He motioned to the landscape, shadowed rock hills on each side. 'Aren't you getting sick of this?'

'No. I don't know. Maybe.' I paused. 'So you've made up your mind.'

'To go?' Mark finally looked at me. 'It's been coming. We both knew it.'

When we returned to the apartment, Mark put the kettle on for tea, then went to the living room to watch TV. I sat on the floor by the door and undid the laces of my black boots, pulling the sides away from the tongue, and forced them off my feet, my bum crunching tracked-in salt. I stood up, brushing grit from my hands and pants, then rubbed my fingers together and put them to my nose. Dried dog spit — a hint of chewed meat.

I entered the spare room and sat at the desk. Surrounding the illustration were cleaned paintbrushes, scraps of towel, watercolour tubes, grainy photocopies of ravens, a mug of muddy water. The mug was an old souvenir: TORONTO with a rainbow behind the CN Tower, stains of dripping colour on its surface. I opened Mark's black binder. *Ravens can be greedy, selfish ... The birds search to slake their appetites (for food or knowledge) ... groups of birds: fleets, flock, murder (crows), unkindness (ravens) ...*

I placed my hand over the painted raven. My hand covered it completely. In the kitchen, the kettle whistled, slow and sweet at first, then louder, persistent, panicked.

'Want tea?' Mark called.

Standing up from the desk, I grabbed the mug and slowly turned it upside down, the brown-grey water spilling, then pooling onto the thick watercolour paper, raven and paper blending, bleeding into a monochrome mess.

'Yeah,' I answered, whirling towards the kitchen. 'Coming.'

You Wouldn't Recognize Me

I woke up upside down. Heard the hiss of the compressing airbag, the *tick, tick* of the turn signal, the *swish, thunk* of the windshield wipers. Then a voice.

'Mom?'

Three weeks later, Walt left and took Zoë. Took, but she chose to go. I see her twice a month only because a judge told her she had to. This weekend will be the first I've been sober. Ten days. Double digits.

Within a half hour of Zoë's arrival, I'm on the phone with Renata.

'She comes in, drops her bag, goes to her room, shuts the door.'

'She's how old?' Renata asks.

'Fifteen,' I say.

'I'm suddenly glad I had three boys.'

'What if I had just a little wine?' I ask. 'Not even a full glass.'

'No Elise,' she says. 'No no no no no. Go knock on her door.'

'I did.'

'Knock again.'

I hang up the phone and climb the stairs to Zoë's room. Renata and I met at Sober Sisters. She told the group that when her boys were young, not long after her separation, she'd take them and a travel mug full of coffee and rum to the park, sit on a bench and get tipsy as they shovelled and slid and spun and howled and tumbled.

'It was like being at the zoo watching the chimps. They're so like us, these boys, yet so different. Wilder and hairier. I loved those afternoons, I didn't want them to end. I didn't want my buzz to end either.'

Outside Zoë's room I can hear her music, the angst-filled wail of a flannel-clad boy, the clash of cymbal and distorted guitar. I knock.

'Knock knock.'

I hear her bedsprings creak and the music gets louder.

'I take it you won't listen,' I call. I step away from the door and walk down the hall. At the stairs I hear Zoë's door click and open. The music has stopped.

'Mom?' Her brown eyes, mostly hidden by her long, black bangs, are wide open. 'Dad won't let me go on the pill.'

I start coughing and my eyes tear up. Zoë blurs and ripples in my vision. She got her period just two years ago.

'Will you talk to him?'

Talk? We haven't talked in weeks. It's Zoë who's done the talking for us, our arbitrator, our go-between. 'Zoë, I —' My voice gets caught so I nod. Oh for a little rum in my coffee. Something warm. The hug I need from the inside. Zoë returns to her room and closes the door. The screaming guitar resumes.

'You could have told me she had a boyfriend,' I say into the phone, which is tucked between my ear and shoulder as I scrounge through the cupboards and fridge for candy or cookies or anything sweet. Quit drinking and your body cries like a baby for ice cream. Last week I spooned Kool-Aid crystals into my mouth. Now I spread peanut butter onto some stale graham crackers.

'I did, Elise. Sometimes you have trouble remembering.'

'Asking for the pill now is better than asking for an abortion later.'

'She's fifteen.'

'I know she's fifteen, Walt.'

'I'm fifteen and a half.' Zoë has entered the kitchen. 'Tell him.'

'I heard her,' Walt says.

I crunch into a graham cracker and offer one to Zoë. She rolls her eyes and takes one, nibbles a corner, then throws it in the garbage.

'The last thing I wanted was to talk about our daughter's sex life,' Walt says. I laugh. Bits of cracker fly out of my mouth. Walt and I barely talked about our own sex life, let alone had one. I was too busy drinking and he was too busy shift-working, then sleeping. Walt never drank. Well, when we were young or once in a while on a hot summer day he'd have a beer, then get a headache and go lie down, leaving me alone, once again, to chase my buzz. I wipe cracker crumbs off the phone.

'Gross, Mom. What's he saying?'

I wave my hand at Zoë and shake my head.

'She's still going to do this,' I say. Then, quietly, 'And it's better this than becoming grandparents.'

'I *do not* want a baby,' Zoë calls out.

'Tell her she still is a baby,' Walt says.

'I heard that and I *am not!* I am fifteen and a *half!*'

'*The boyfriend is nineteen.*'

'*Nineteen!*' *I swallow a lump of peanut butter and scowl at Zoë.*

'Mom, Dad is *six* years older than you!'

'It's different when you're older,' I say.

'Well, I can't *fucking* wait till I'm *older* and fucking outta here!' And with that, Zoë spins out of the kitchen and stomps up the stairs to her room, slamming her door. All the walls rattle.

'Did she just swear at you?' Walt asks.

'It wasn't quite at me.'

'She's lucky I'm not there.'

I sigh. Walt sighs. It's the most we've talked since they moved out. Hell, it's the most we've talked since we *were* living together. Amazing how much you can say to someone when there's no TV, no kids, no alcohol, no screaming, no throwing. Amazing, too, how I can forget our bad enough to miss our good.

'She's only getting older, Walt. She's going to swear, she's going to wear what she wants and she's going to have sex. Our job is to keep talking to her or else she'll also grow farther away.'

Walt coughs, then is quiet.

'Zoë says you've stopped drinking?'

'Eleven days sober.'

'If you can quit drinking, Elise, you can also talk to our daughter.'

After I flipped the car, I reached to turn off the signal. I couldn't open the car door. The airbag and seat belt had me pinned.

'Mom?'

My voice came through a mouthful of hair.

'We're upside down,' I told my daughter.

'We've been that way for a while,' she said.

I have a couple of conditions. One: I meet the boyfriend. Two: She comes to a couple of my Sober Sisters meetings. She's thinking about it, up in her room, music going, door closed. I'd like to hear less music. See the door open. They forget that we were kids too. I remember. I remember how much I wanted to have sex and what I did to get it. Lucky Walt. I remember because it's how I feel right now about booze.

I bike to the Y for my meeting. Losing booze, losing my licence, nearly losing my family, my life, I've lost almost seven pounds. Booze wouldn't recognize me if booze saw me.

Renata finds me waiting on the steps for Zoë.

'I bought my oldest son condoms. Imagine being in the heat of it, opening up a condom wrapper, then hearing your mom's voice as you're trying to slide it on. Poor kid.'

We look up as a red-and-fluorescent-green Chevette sputters up to the curb.

'I should have known her father wouldn't drop her off.'

Renata grabs my wrist and leans quickly to my ear.

'Is being sober suddenly making you very horny?'

'Renata!' I'm watching Zoë step from the car. She's wearing black tights, black high-top sneakers, a green skirt and a blue hoodie. She has a new green streak in her hair. 'Like teenager-horny? Almost. I'm thinking about it more than I have in some time. It's all this pill talk. Just because she's suddenly sexually active doesn't mean I have to be sexually *in*active, right?'

Renata lets go of my wrist.

'Where else can we pick up men besides bars?'

'How long will this be?' Zoë calls up the steps.

'We'll be done by eight thirty,' I say. She says something into the car, then closes the door. The car rattles and grumbles away.

I introduce Renata and Zoë, then we head into the basement of the Y. The smell of chlorine and warm Styrofoam cups, chemical, false, nauseating, has become the smell of sobriety. Of course sobriety would never smell like fresh-cut grass or patchouli, even though Renata asked the facilitator if we could burn incense at the meetings. No way. Bonnie, the facilitator, is a stern, old, boxy grey-haired nurse who misses the days of starched caps and carbolic soap. She gives Renata and me something to talk about after the meetings.

We get coffee and tea and sit in a circle. Zoë sits five chairs away. Fine. If she wants to pretend she's not my daughter I can pretend I'm not her mom. I've tried too hard not to look like one. I haven't shorn my long hair into a convenient stub, I haven't traded my cotton and wool for polyester and Christmas sweaters. I could drink most fathers under the table. Maybe I shouldn't be proud of that one.

We begin each meeting by holding hands and repeating the ten Sober Sisters proclamations: no more drinking, forget the past, embrace the love, etc., etc. It's hokey, but a million times better than AA's focus on God. How dare God be a part of sobriety — he changed water into wine! So many addicts replace one addiction with another: cigarettes, caffeine, food, religion. Looking outside when we should be looking in. And, God? It's not the drunks at the bar that are responsible for these holy wars. Well, maybe they do some name-calling. But those slugs usually come with hugs.

The meeting progresses. We talk about quitting, we talk about staying quit, we talk about our families, our jobs, how good and, mostly, how bad we feel. We nod and pass out tissues. Zoë sits blankly, wiggling her feet, chewing her fingernails, just like her father. Then Leslie says, 'I think it's great that Elise's daughter is here to support her.' Others murmur in agreement. I look at Zoë. She scowls.

'Mom made me,' she says.

'She made you?' Bonnie repeats.

'Why?' asks Renata, who knows exactly why.

Zoë frowns and lowers her head. Her hair falls around her face. She mutters something.

'We didn't quite catch that,' says Bonnie.

'It's a bargain,' Zoë says. 'I don't, like, live with her anymore.'

'We know,' says Marilyn.

'My kids live with my mother,' says Leslie.

Zoë's quiet. I'm quieter.

'A bargain?' Renata asks, grinning.

Neither of us says anything. Then, finally, Bonnie looks at me and says, 'Elise?'

'Because Zoë's underage she needs my consent to go on the pill. I had a couple of conditions.'

'The *pill*,' Marilyn stage-whispers.

'Mom!' Zoë whines, turning red.

'She's too young,' Marilyn says.

'You're still not safe,' Renata says. 'A condom —'

'I told my kids, no sex, not until you're eighteen,' Patsy interrupts.

'They're still gonna do it,' Renata says. 'Heck, they may be doing it right now.'

'Oh no, no way.' Patsy crosses her arms.

'Was it your boyfriend's idea?' Leslie asks. 'I went on the pill at seventeen, went off, went on, got pregnant. Don't go on and off it, dear. It'll mess up your periods. It will improve your acne, though. That was the best part.' Leslie looks at the group. 'I'm envious that Elise has a daughter who's not sneaking around or lying or —'

'Or acting like a drunk?' Renata chimes in. 'Maybe she learned by example.' Renata raises her eyebrows at me.

'How did your mom's drinking make you feel?' Bonnie suddenly asks.

Zoë crosses her legs, puts a fingertip in her mouth. She sucked her thumb for a long time. Would we be closer now if I'd breastfed? She looks around at all the ladies. Where'd she get her confidence? I'd have been under my chair at her age.

'I, uh —' She begins to bite her fingernail again. I look at her and shake my head. She scowls, then says, very quietly, 'I hate her.' Ouch. The ladies shift and murmur.

'You don't feel that way,' Patsy says.

'You girls always hate your mothers,' Marilyn says. 'You won't hate her forever.'

'She almost killed me!' Zoë says. I nod. I almost did. The ladies are quiet for a long time. They know all about the accident. Many of them have had close calls themselves: fights, blackouts, suicide attempts.

Bonnie asks, 'Do you hate your mother, sitting here, right now, the one who's sixteen days sober, or do you hate the mother who got in the car accident?'

'Aren't they both the same?'

'Are they?'

Renata hands me a tissue. I blow my nose and try not to vomit.

'I don't know what I feel right now. She's, like, not the same mom.'

I find Zoë outside after the meeting. It's raining, heavy and thick and slow, ready to turn to snow.

'Well —' I start. Zoë is looking towards the road where she was dropped off.

'What's his name?' I ask.

'Oh. Uh — there he is!' She runs towards the little red-and-green car.

'Zoë!' I call after her. Opening the passenger door, she looks up. 'Thanks for coming. It was —' What was it? Great? Helpful? Depressing? Sobering. 'I appreciated it.'

She waves and gets in the car but they don't speed away. It idles for a minute or two as I unlock my bike and wrap the lock around the frame. I'm about to pedal away when I hear Zoë's voice.

'Mom? Digger wants to know if you want a ride.'

Digger. I'm curious. I'm also already soaked and cold. I wheel my bike around to the back of his car. Digger hops out and opens the hatch.

'It'll fit?' I ask.

Digger bends and releases the front tire from the frame, then lifts the heavy bike and squeezes everything into the back of his car. The belts and clasps on his leather jacket clang and clatter.

'Voilà,' he says, opening the back door and standing at attention like a chauffeur while I slide in. The car smells like old socks and stale cigarettes. As we pull away from the curb, Zoë pops a tape into the player, but Digger turns the volume down and gives her a look. Interesting. Zoë crosses her arms and, sighing, turns towards her window. I stare at the back of Digger's head. His hair is clipped short, except at the crown, where it is long, and pushed floppily over his forehead.

'Roads are dirty,' Digger says. I assume he means messy, slippery, as the rain is definitely snow now, thick and white. Dirty? Who is this boy who wants to fuck my daughter? Is he wearing eyeliner?

'How did you two meet?' I ask.

'At the mall,' Zoë says.

'I came up to her, just like that, and told her she's beautiful.'

'When I walked away he shouted out, "I love you!" Then he found me later and, like, gave me his number.'

'And you called,' I say.

'Why not?' Zoë shrugs.

Just like that.

'You're going to the college?'

'Yup. For animation.'

'Like cartoons?'

'Mom! God. It's not just cartoons.'

'It's computers, it's life drawing, it's special effects. It's also very long and very tedious. I made a little thing where a ball rolls into a hole and it took me three days for a fifteen-second clip. I'm a bit faster now.'

Life drawing. Isn't that nude models? Does Zoë pose for this guy? Naked? The windows are fogging up. I trace a circle, a few lines onto the window. It turns into a stick man. I connect his two stick feet and make a triangular skirt. Now it's a stick woman. I was an artist too. A con artist, an escape artist. With one stroke of my hand, I wipe the stick woman away. Sixteen days sober — what the hell am I now?

'Without drinking, what are we supposed to do with all this extra time?'

Renata's dropping me off after our Saturday-night coffee.

'I've been biking a lot,' I say. ''Course I have to. You?'

'My on-again, off-again seems to be on again. He was over last Sunday. He wants me to get rid of the wine bottles in the garage. I need the reminder. He swears he won't come back — he hates the bottles, hates my son, loves my tits.' Renata shrugs. I look at her chest. What a rack!

We sit in her car and stare at my dark house. Zoë has gone out. I told Renata about our visit to Dr Corrigan yesterday.

'How do family doctors go from chicken pox to strep throat to pap smears in just a few years?'

'Doctors?' says Renata. 'How do we go from diapers to cuddles to sex to "fuck yous" in just a few more?'

'I was so happy to go on the pill,' I say. 'I wasn't convinced I wanted to be a mother. But drinking made me forget to take it. At least being pregnant forced me to stop drinking. Mostly.'

'The pill was a huge deal,' Renata says. 'Now it's nothing. Just part of growing up.'

'Girls today slide out of their thongs without realizing how good they have it,' I say.

'Then, sex was just sex. Now it's chlamydia, it's AIDS.'

'Houses, husbands, kids. We ended up the same as our moms. Except we kept our jobs and had orgasms.' I sigh. 'Lately I'm seeing Zoë through the wrong end of a telescope.'

'She came to you for the pill. She could have used condoms.

Obviously, her door's open a crack. Stick your foot in there before she closes it all the way.'

I switch on the kitchen light. Funny how quickly I find it when all I have is caffeine in my system. Once it's on I see Zoë's sneakers and a pair of large black boots by the door, so either Zoë and Digger went out in March in stocking feet, or they're in the house. Somewhere. Doing … No. I clang pots and run water. Open the fridge then close it loudly. Turn on the radio. I wait. Nothing. Sighing, I make my way upstairs. Zoë's door is slightly ajar, her music quiet. A pale light shines into the hallway. I hear her bedsprings creak as I tiptoe towards the door. I see her head at the foot of her bed. I see her fingers in her mouth, her knees are bent, her pants at her ankles. And between her legs, my daughter's legs, is Digger's crazy, flopping hair swaying back and forth. I gasp. He looks up and right at me. His eyes focus. He looks away. He *is* wearing eyeliner. Zoë turns her head.

'Mom?' She pulls at her pants and reaches towards the door. 'Oh shit. Shit!' And slams it. I watch her purple DO NOT DISTURB sign swing and rattle against her doorknob. The sign she made when she was twelve. I watch it, I keep watching it until it slows and is still. I blink. I need to wash my eyes, scrub my brain. Get pie-eyed, blind, blotto. I rush down to the kitchen, grab my coat, leave the house, jump on my bike and start riding.

At the kitchen door, just before the accident, Zoë appeared after I dropped my keys.

'Here,' she said, picking them up.

'Where'd you come from?' I asked, fumbling through my jacket for the armhole.

'It's inside-out,' she said.

I nodded, turning it right-side out.

'Where you going?' she asked.

'I have some errands.' I checked my wallet for cash.

'I'm coming,' she said, pulling on her coat.

'No,' I said. 'I shouldn't even be driving.' By the time I finished my sentence, she was already in the driveway.

There are five liquor stores in town and I know them all. The renovated one in the north end with the fancy wine section. The two attached to grocery stores — how convenient! The rundown south-end store with its working-class, quitting-time clientele. And this one, right downtown, open later than the rest. It was here I was heading the night I nearly killed Zoë, and it's here I'm now standing, straddling my bike, my fingers turning numb in the cold air.

Twenty minutes until closing. Nineteen.

Eighteen.

Eighteen steps to the door. Seventeen. Thirteen. Nine.

The door chimes and I nod to the cashier. She nods back. Everyone knows your name! The smell of the store, like all liquor stores, is intoxicating enough: icy and medicinal. Sweet healing booze. In the summer I stood in the giant, walk-in beer fridge. Cooled down before buying my coolers.

I head straight for the cleansing gin. I run my fingers along the bottles. Clear bottle. Green bottle. Blue bottle. Liquid jewels, contained in glass. *Break in case of emergency.*

'We close in ten minutes,' the cashier calls out. I can hear her counting coins. I nod. I grab a green bottle. Surprised to feel no guilt, I take two. I turn around quickly and snatch — what is it? Wine. Chardonnay. Two. Three! I need a cart. I waddle up to the front. A green bottle starts to slip. I thrust my knee forward and catch it, just as the other green bottle inches towards the floor. The cashier stops counting her coins.

'Ma'am, I — Alan!' I see the manager's head appear in his raised office window. He comes running down the stairs.

'Hold on!' he calls.

Too late. It's the wine that goes, then the gin. They slip slowly but smash quickly and loudly onto the linoleum floor. Glass is everywhere. Green glass. Clear glass. Glass and liquid. What a gas. I start laughing. The fumes alone must be getting me high. Suddenly there's a hand on my elbow.

'Here you go,' Alan says, taking the other bottles, leading me away from the mess. My wet shoes crunch in the glass. Bits get stuck in the soles. Alan sits me on the stairs.

'I'm so sorry,' I say. 'I'll pay.' I start to get up. 'I'll help clean up.'

'We're taking care of it,' Alan says, and, indeed, the cashier has a mop and bucket. She is bent over the mess, picking up the larger chunks of glass.

'Be careful,' I say. She glares at me and carries the glass to the garbage.

'Is there someone I can call?' Alan asks.

'I have my bike,' I say, pulling a piece of glass from my shoe.

'I do still have to call,' he says. He thinks I'm drunk. Ha! I wish. It's not his fault. I smell like I am. And, of course, I've been drunk here before.

'Yes,' I say. 'Yes. There is someone you can call.'

Walt, my hero, my prince in blue jeans and a shining pickup. How many times have you rescued me? It all started over twenty years ago: me, a near-virginal bride with a developing addiction, you, my still-thin, newly employed groom. Driving off into the sunrise, not the sunset.

'And you thought you'd hung up your spurs. No more damsels in distress.'

'What are you talking about?' Walt gives me the look, quickly, from the driver's seat. I can hear my bike squeaking and sliding around in the back of his truck.

'No, not *that* look. That's only for when I'm drunk.'

'You smell like you are.'

'In a bottle, in the body, alcohol always lets you know it's around.' I turn his radio on, flip to a classic rock station, then turn it off. 'This wagon ride's a bumpy one,' I finally say.

'I can't get mad anymore,' he says. 'I'm not going to fight.'

'Shut me out then. Walt the conscientious objector. Walt the draft dodger. It's what you do best. Work, TV, silence. I yelled to get through your friggen walls.' I move my hand up and down between us. Yup, that wall's still there, solid as ever. He grabs my hand and pushes it back to my side of the truck.

'Your hand is freezing.'

'I forgot my gloves.'

I tell him why I left the house so quickly. Why I was at the liquor store. After more silence I say, 'Do you remember our first time?'

'Barely.' He grins.

'I can count how many times I've seen you that drunk. Wasn't my first time.'

Walt stops smiling.

'Wait. What do you mean?'

'First time drunk. Wait. Oh!' I sit up straighter. 'You thought I meant first *time*. Oh no. It was. My first time. It's why I remember so clearly. Ouch!'

'I wonder if anyone has ever lost their hymen to a guy named Hyman?'

I laugh, then say, 'I know someone who has to a boy named Digger.'

Walt shakes his head, then laughs too.

'Turn it off, Zoë.'

Zoë looks at me, then back to the TV.

'You heard your mother.' Walt comes into the room. Zoë's eyes widen, surprised to see her father. I am too. Walt sits in a chair and I sit beside Zoë on the couch, as if he's about to scold us both.

'Look, if you didn't want me to do it, why'd Mom take me to the doctor?'

'We don't want you to do it,' I say, 'just like we don't want you to swear or smoke or drive. You will, though, you are, so we'll enrol you in driver's ed. and make sure you don't get pregnant. You still live under this roof—'

'Yeah, and I live over this basement. I live between these walls. Isn't that the contract? Aren't I still, like, a minor? Aren't I *supposed* to live under this roof?'

'A contract goes both ways. You get your room, your space, this TV, food. We get to know we're not coming home to a porno.'

'Gross.'

'Yes, gross. I don't want you alone with him here and your father wants the same at his place.'

'Digger has his own apartment! What's the difference?'

'It's his apartment,' Walt finally says. 'This is ours — your mom's. Mine.'

'Ooooh!' Zoë stomps her feet. She's been doing this for years. No extra cookie. Can't stay up late. Stomped feet. Red face. 'I'll move out! I will!'

'You do and we'll have him arrested.'

'What?! For what?'

'You're fifteen. He's nineteen. We can do this, Zoë, and we will.'

'Zoë,' I say. 'We've given you a lot already. You can't have everything.'

Zoë's face is glowing red. Her eyes are bulging with tears.

'No,' she says to me. 'You owe me. You fucking owe me.'

'Yes. Yes I do. By getting sober. By getting sober and being able to stand my ground. By not disappearing, again, into a bottle. By not letting some boy take my place.'

'Dad!'

'Go to your room, Zo. The conversation's over.'

Zoë squeezes her hands into fists. She bolts from the couch and flies up the stairs to her room. Her door slams, the walls shudder, and I can hear, once again, the DO NOT DISTURB sign spinning and spinning and spinning.

By noon the next day Zoë still hasn't emerged from her room. I climb the stairs with toast and orange juice, then stand and stare at her door. It stares blankly back. I finger the sign that hangs from the doorknob, then lift it off and flip it over. COME IN! it now says. I knock and enter.

Zoë, lying in bed, turns her face towards the wall.

'Brunch,' I say, laying the plate and glass on her nightstand. Pushing shirts and pants off her desk chair, I take a seat. I study her wall, where she has taped dozens of pictures of wild-haired boys and angry girls in rock bands, on bikes, in cars, in wheat fields and abandoned factories, surrounded by pages from comic books, slogans and headlines and bumper stickers: QUESTION AUTHORITY, VEGETARIANS TASTE BETTER, HUG A TREE, GIVE PEACE A CHANCE, FUCK OFF AND DIE.

'You just gonna sit there?' Zoë asks, muffled, into her pillow.

'Yup. All day. Soon I'll eat your toast.'

Zoë shrugs. Somehow she gets her whole body to shrug.

'Zoë —' I start. 'Why'd you come with me the night I flipped the car? You didn't have to. I didn't ask …'

I hear Zoë sniff. Finally she turns around. She grabs the toast and sits up. She eats slowly, even the crust, staring ahead the whole time. I stare at her wall. FUCK OFF AND DIE. FUCK OFF AND DIE. FUCK OFF —

'Because,' she finally says, putting her empty plate down. 'Because I, like, had to.'

She gives me a look, different from her father's, not angry or accusing, yet just as familiar: sad, disappointed. A mother's look.

'I didn't need you to take care of me.'

'No? Who called 911? Who got you to bed when I'd find you on the bathroom floor?'

I get off the chair and sit on her bed. I reach out and brush her bangs out of her eyes. She lets me. I put my hand on top of hers. Amazing how quickly these hands grew, how quickly, just like the rest of her. Hands, legs, toes, breasts, hips. Everything growing up and away.

'I'm changing,' I finally say.

'So am I.' She cups her breasts and laughs.

Digger's knocking on the door. He's agreed to drive us to the next Sober Sisters meeting. When I come into the kitchen they are kissing.

'Gross! Cut it out!' I say, opening the fridge for a bottle of water. Zoë mumbles sorry and Digger looks away. He is reaching for something behind his back.

'Zoë wanted me to give you this,' he says, handing me a small but heavy canvas. I flip it over. It's a painting of Zoë — the back of her shoulders, her turned neck, the edge of her scowling profile. The paint is thick and dark and sketchy but it's still her looking at me.

'It's beautiful,' I say.

'It's just a quick study. Zoë won't pose. She gets bored.'

'I get sore,' she says, coming to look at the painting with me. 'Some part of me always goes numb.'

I prop it up on the kitchen table and step back.

'It's like she's about to say something,' I say. 'What?'

'She did say something.' Digger chuckles. 'What was it?'

'Fuck off,' Zoë says, grinning proudly.

Acknowledgements

The author gratefully acknowledges the recognition and financial support of the Ontario Arts Council, the province of Nova Scotia through the Department of Communities, Culture and Heritage and the Writers' Trust of Canada (for administering the Bronwen Wallace Award).

Slightly different versions of the following stories have appeared in various periodicals: 'High-Water Mark' (*The New Quarterly* and *The Journey Prize Stories 19*); 'Mona Says Fire, Fire, Fire' and 'You Wouldn't Recognize Me' (*The New Quarterly*); 'Happy Meat' (*Grain*); and 'Diving for Pearls' (*The Fiddlehead*).

Thanks also to Kim Jernigan and *The New Quarterly;* The Saskatchewan Writers' Guild (for enabling me to write 'Saudade' at their St. Peter's Abbey Writers' Retreat); Chandra Wohleber (for her invaluable edits, suggestions and support); and Darryl Whetter, my first reader.

About the Author

Nicole Dixon has lived in Toronto, Sarnia, Windsor, North Bay and Halifax. Her stories have been nominated for the Journey Prize, short-listed for a CBC Literary Award and have appeared in *The New Quarterly, Grain, The Fiddlehead* and *Canadian Notes & Queries*. In 2005 she won the Writers' Trust of Canada RBC Bronwen Wallace Award for short fiction. Nicole is electronic resources librarian at Cape Breton University. She divides her time between New Waterford, Cape Breton, and Advocate Harbour, Nova Scotia.

A Note on the Type

This book is typeset in Junius. The typeface is named for Franciscus Junius, a pioneer of Germanic philology who was born at Heidelberg in 1591.

The typeface was digitized in the early 1990s from the Pica Saxon used to print Georges Hickes' *Thesaurus* (Oxford: Sheldonian Theatre, 1703–05). Junius is primarily designed for use by medievalists, and is readily available for download from the English Department at the University of Virginia.

The display type is Clarendon Condensed, which appeared in *Specimens of Wood Type* (Wells & Webb, 1854).